THE FEAR AND MEOW

A WHISKERS AND WORDS MYSTERY
BOOK EIGHT

ERYN SCOTT

KRISTOPHERSON
PRESS
Publishing

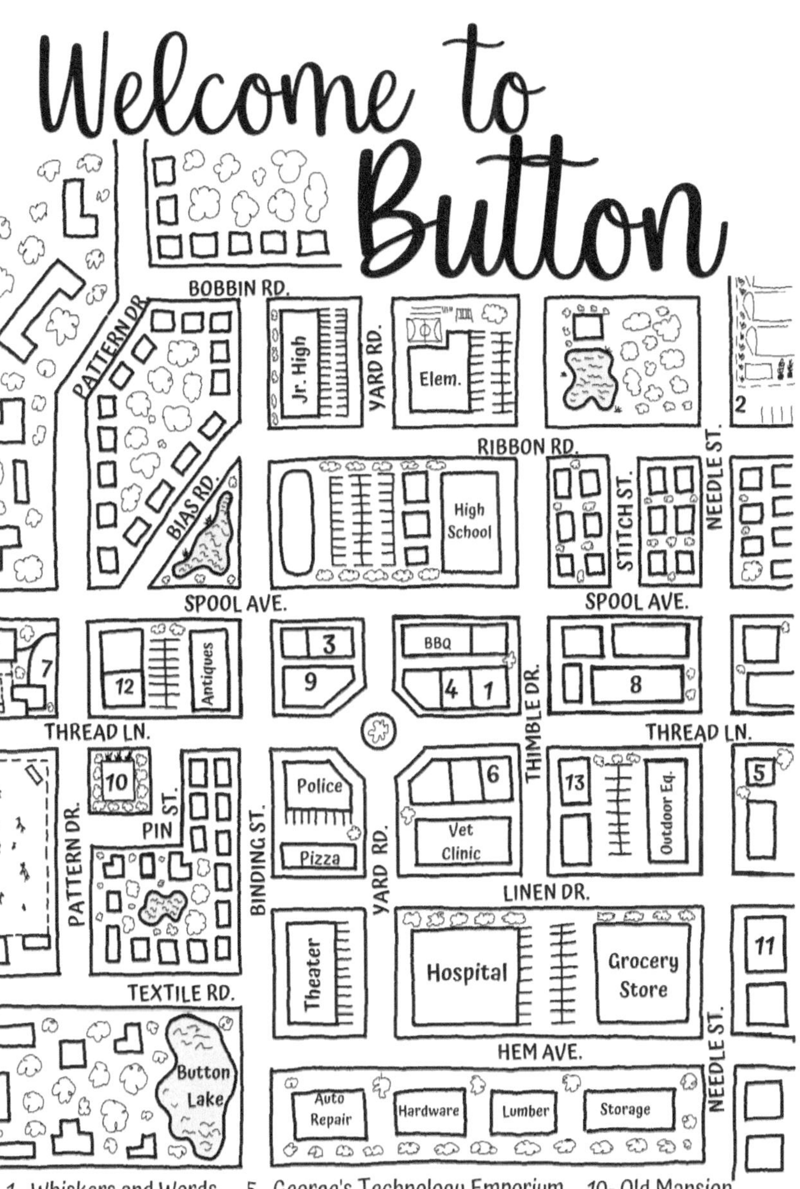

1 - Whiskers and Words

2 - Willow's Nursery

3 - Button Bistro

4 - Scoop O' Button

5 - George's Technology Emporium

6 - Bean and Button Coffeehouse

7 - Willow and Easton's houses

8 - Material Girls

9 - The Upholstered Button

10 - Old Mansion

11 - Bank

12 - Pet Store

13 - Bakery

CHAPTER 1

Louisa Henry stopped halfway up the staircase, setting down the large suitcase for a moment to give her arms a break. She swiped the back of her hand across her forehead before hoisting her friend's luggage up once more and tottering the rest of the way to her apartment.

"Lo-ou, I could've gotten that on my next trip," George complained as she clomped up behind Lou, setting down a cat carrier and another, smaller suitcase. Any exasperation in the young woman's voice was half-hearted, however, overshadowed by gratitude as she glanced around the apartment. "You're letting me stay here. You shouldn't have to move my stuff too."

Lou rolled the suitcase over to the spare bedroom. "I definitely thought it was going to be lighter when I decided to bring it up," she admitted with a chuckle. Then, peering at the suitcase, she asked, "Did you decide to bring *all* the rocks from your yard?"

George let her head fall back in a laugh. "Believe it or not, most of the heavy stuff in there is Geralt's." She motioned to the cat carrier, where a gray-and-white cat peered out at the new space. Cupping a hand around one side of her mouth, George whispered, "He's kind of a diva."

Lou believed it. While the cat was as sweet as could be, Geralt demanded to be close to his owner as much as possible. It had gotten to the point where George had started strapping him into a cloth baby carrier so she could bring him around with her while she worked or went on with her day.

More footsteps clomped up the stairs, and a man strode into the apartment, carrying a suitcase in each hand. "Did you borrow one of these from every person in town?" Noah asked as he set down the luggage. "There's no way you own this many suitcases."

He was much less winded than Lou had been. Whereas her strengths lay in running, Noah's muscled arms and broad shoulders had made easy work of the heavy bags.

George rolled her eyes at him as she took inventory of the bags surrounding her. "You try moving your life and business somewhere else for two whole weeks, but yes, I borrowed most of these."

The discovery of termites in George's house had been stressful enough, knowing it was something she would have to take care of in order to save the integrity of the structure. When she found out she would have to be out of the space while they fumigated it, she added worries about the technology support business she ran out of her residence to the list.

Lou hadn't hesitated to invite George and Geralt to come live with her and the myriad of rescue cats who called her bookstore, Whiskers and Words, home. And while the fumigation process would be over in a matter of days, they'd decided George should extend her stay to two weeks so she could finally replace the old carpet in her home with wood floors. She'd been saving up for the renovation for years, but had put it off since it would mean closing her business for the duration of the project.

Noah held up his hands in defeat, proving such a move wouldn't be easy for him either. He sent a dimpled smile over at Lou, who flushed at the attention. She quickly schooled her expression back into something less adoring, in case George looked her way.

George, along with the rest of the people in Button—save for Lou's best friend—were unaware that the two had started a romantic relationship. It wasn't as if they were ashamed. Noah had been divorced for two years, and Lou had been a widow for almost as long. But Noah's daughter was already incredibly attached to Lou, and they'd wanted to make sure it was going to stick before letting Marigold know it was happening.

With a nosy town like Button, they found it easier to keep it a secret until they were sure.

Lou's gaze skirted over the handsome man, her heart speeding up in the lovely way it did whenever she looked at him.

"This is the first time you've been up here, isn't it?" George asked Noah.

Coughing in surprise, Noah cleared his throat and nodded. It *should've* been. It *would've* been if the two of them hadn't been sneaking around together. But they'd spent a lot of time up there together over the past few months. Lou's place was usually the safer of the two since Noah lived in a residential neighborhood, and Lou lived above her bookshop in the middle of the business district downtown. There were less prying eyes downtown that might catch Noah sneaking into Lou's apartment on nights when he didn't have his daughter.

Turning serious, George waved a hand toward Lou. "But you two really don't need to help me with all of this. You've got the shop open downstairs, Lou."

George was right. Even though one of Lou's bookshop regulars was watching over the register for her while she helped George with her suitcases, she probably shouldn't dally too long.

"Okay. Well, I'll see you down there whenever you're ready." Lou motioned to the space. "Make yourself at home."

"Thanks for your help." George dipped her head toward Noah. "Both of you," she added before disappearing into the spare bedroom to start the unpacking process.

Noah and Lou started down the stairs but paused at the same place where Lou had stopped for a break on the way up. Noah, in front of Lou, pivoted until he was facing her. His strong arms wrapped around her at the same time she let her hands snake around the back of his neck. Their lips met in a kiss that made Lou's whole body feel lighter.

Noah pulled her closer, breathing her in like he couldn't get enough of her. She knew the feeling.

As much as Lou didn't want their embrace to end, there wasn't a door between them and George, like there was leading into the bookshop below. If George came down the staircase, she would run right into them and their secret would be … well, not so secret anymore.

Lou wasn't sure that George knowing would be the worst thing, though. She was sure the young woman could keep the information to herself. But it was Noah's daughter and his decision to make.

Their eyes met in the dim light of the staircase. Noah tilted his head forward in response to the unspoken reminder that had passed between them. They needed to let the town know, and soon. As much fun as it had been sneaking around, it was getting more complicated—especially with George moving in—and they were ready to let people in on their relationship.

"I'll figure out a time that we can sit down with Cass this week," Noah whispered.

They'd both agreed that Noah's ex-wife needed to be the first person they told. Noah knew how unsettling it felt to hear about Cassidy's new relationships through others in the town, and he didn't want to put her through that. The fact that he was being so considerate of Cassidy, when his ex-wife hadn't afforded him the same courtesy, only further proved to Lou what a thoughtful person he was. Plus, Lou wasn't from the surrounding towns like Cassidy's men had been. Lou was an integral member of the small community of Button, where Cassidy lived and worked. They felt she deserved a moment to get used to the idea before the rest of the town.

Stealing one more kiss, Lou said, "This week. Sounds good. Until then, where should we meet?"

"I feel like teenagers." Noah's chuckle was deep and made Lou want to press her face against his chest to get the full rumbly effect. He inhaled. "Oh, that actually gives me an idea." When Lou cocked her head in question, Noah said, "Back in high school, a bunch of people would use the northern entrance to Forest Pond as a *date* spot. The community mostly hangs out on the southern end of the lake by the dock."

Noise from the apartment above made Lou check over her shoulder. "Forest Pond. Tonight." Her mouth spread into an excited grin.

With that, the two quietly crept down the rest of the stairs, hoping not to alert George to the fact that they were only now moving into the bookshop. The smell of freshly printed pages and crisply made covers met Lou as they stepped into the warm space.

Outside the windows, an icy wind snapped through the trees, pushing big gray clouds across the sky only to be replaced with darker ones. Lou didn't mind the blustery weather when she had the coziest bookshop around. In fact, stormy days often brought some of her best sales figures, as customers lingered longer in the comfortable space. A fire crackled in the woodstove in the front corner. Each of her rescue cats curled up close to the hearth so they might soak up its heat.

Along with the soft lighting throughout the space, the quiet sound of conversation added to the warmth of the bookshop. Lou's regulars chatted happily, pulling other customers into their discussions from time to time.

Forrest, a local psychologist who spent his time between patients reading and showering the rescue cats with scratches and pets, stood behind the register. He'd volunteered to watch the place for her while she helped George.

Seeing that she'd returned, Forrest ducked his head, vacated the place behind the shop computer, and reclaimed his spot on the love seat in the sitting area. Just as Lou stepped behind the computer, the door swung open, and an older woman blew into the shop like a gust of wind.

"You won't believe it," said the woman, another of Lou's regulars, named Cricket. "They're going through with that meeting of theirs right now," she scoffed. "I saw them arriving as I left my house just now."

If her agitated state hadn't been clear from her clipped tone, the exasperated way she struggled out of the mustard-colored scarf that had been wrapped around her neck cemented her frustration. That annoyance was directed at a group called the Button Beautification Society, led by Cricket's backyard neighbor Godfrey Crane. They'd been ruffling feathers throughout town since their inaugural meeting last month. So much so that a large group of locals had called for their organization to disband during the previous town meeting. It sounded as though the group would not comply, instead moving forward, hoping to turn an idea into a measure on the next town ballot.

"They're still just a committee with a petition," Noah reminded her softly. "Their measure can still be voted down at the next meeting."

"If we have enough votes on our side," Cricket sniffed. "And that's not even the full truth. That dreadful Godfrey Crane already has too much power in our neighborhood."

Noah couldn't argue with that. Cricket lived in the same Forest Pond neighborhood they had just been discussing on the stairs. Godfrey had recently halted construction on a previously abandoned mansion across the street, claiming everything from noise violations to calling the owner's building permits into question.

"How's Brock handling the work stoppage?" Noah leaned against the fantasy bookshelf.

Cricket clicked her tongue. "I'm not sure that he is. When I left for the quilt shop just now, his crew was hammering away once again."

"I'm sure Godfrey loved that." Forest shook his head. "People ignoring him makes him feel the most powerless." The psychologist glanced up and then added, "I'm guessing." He had to say things like that to keep everyone unsure about whether he was seeing a person as a patient or not.

Expression souring, as if she'd just taken a bite of rotten fruit, Cricket said, "That man is everything wrong with this town, and I wouldn't be sad if he was never allowed to say another word."

Noah stepped forward, placing a gentle hand on Cricket's shoulder. As his mother's best friend, the woman was family to him, and even he could see she'd gotten herself worked up.

Flinching at the touch at first, Cricket's posture softened as she recognized it was Noah. "Well, I should get to the quilt shop. I've got an embroidery class at eleven."

"I'll walk with you," Noah said. "I've got an appointment coming up." His veterinary clinic was in the opposite direction of his family's quilt shop, but Lou knew he would likely walk her all the way there before heading back to his clinic.

Before leaving, Noah cut a quick glance over at Lou. The almost imperceptible twitch of his eyebrows as he did so was as much of a "see you later" as they could allow until the town knew.

Lou checked on Forrest to make sure the psychologist hadn't also caught the look. The man already had his nose buried in his book, however, his fingers scrunching into the gray fur of Anne Mice, who'd abandoned the fireplace to join him on the love seat. Silas, her other regular, hadn't arrived yet. And so, her secret was still safe.

Sighing in relief, Lou focused on a customer who approached the counter with a stack of books in her arms and a smile on her face. The sound of footsteps upstairs chronicled George's progress unpacking throughout the rest of the afternoon.

NOAH AND LOU didn't have to wait long for the cover of darkness to assist with their plans to rendezvous by Forest

Pond that evening. The sun set before dinnertime during November in the Pacific Northwest. So, when Noah texted that he was heading to Easton's just after Lou and George finished eating and were stacking their dinner plates in the dishwasher, she was ready.

The town wouldn't think twice about Noah's truck parked at Easton's house, and Lou's car was an almost constant staple at her best friend's house next door to Easton. Given that both Easton and Willow knew about the relationship, the other couple was the perfect cover.

Lou closed the dishwasher, glancing over at George. "I, uh, thought I might go to Willow's for a bit," she said. "Give you the evening here by yourself to settle in," she added quickly, knowing George might very well try to tag along if Willow's house was the destination.

George yawned. "Sounds good. Cricket might stop by with her new phone later. She said she needs help transferring her photos."

"Great. See you later." Lou grabbed her winter jacket and waved over her shoulder. Then she jogged downstairs and out the back door to her car.

Noah's truck was already at Easton's house when Lou pulled into Willow's driveway, which meant he was probably already in the woods waiting for her. They'd texted their friends a heads-up about parking, so Lou didn't even knock on Willow's door before she checked the road for cars and jogged across toward the Forest Pond neighborhood.

The moon was close to full, so she didn't need her flashlight to find the pathway that ran through the woods in between Cricket's and Godfrey Crane's houses. Just as she entered the forest, Noah stepped out from behind a rhododendron, smiling conspiratorially, like he really was a teenager sneaking out after curfew.

He threaded her fingers through his, warming her already chilly fingertips with his palm. Then he seemed to want to be even closer because he wrapped an arm around her shoulders and tucked her under his arm.

"How was the rest of your day?" Lou asked, staring up at his handsome face in the moonlight.

"Good. How is George settling in?"

"All of her stuff is unpacked." Lou jerked her shoulders in a shrug. "She didn't let me do much."

Even though being alone allowed them to kiss each other without worrying that the townspeople would see, the true draw behind their clandestine meetings was the ability to talk for hours without anyone asking questions or reading into their body language. With the way they gazed into each other's eyes and grinned, it wouldn't take much to figure out what was happening between them. Lou's parents and closest friends had all picked up on the signs well before she had, and that had been back when Lou and Noah were still just friends.

As they walked, the small trail branched to the right and left. Noah guided them right, closer to Godfrey and Diana Crane's home rather than Cricket and Peter Marshall's. Of the two residences, the people in the Marshall home were more likely to recognize Lou and Noah.

But as they passed the Cranes', a floodlight illuminated a figure slumped against the deck railing. It was much too cold out for someone to sit out on their deck, and the figure wasn't in one of the chairs nearby. Lou's worry ratcheted up as she noticed the person wasn't moving.

Noah ran forward, cutting through the forest to the Cranes' backyard. Lou followed close behind, her phone already out and a call ringing through to 9-1-1.

The man's white polo was stained red, a gun sat in his lap, and a handkerchief covered his face. Even with the cloth covering his features, it was plain enough to see that the man in front of them was none other than Godfrey Crane, the leader of the Button Beautification Society. If there had been any doubt, red lettering scribbled across the handkerchief read *Stop the Vote*.

CHAPTER 2

Noah probably didn't need to check for a pulse, given the rest of the clues at the scene, but he did anyway. Shaking his head, he met Lou's eyes. "He's gone. His body's cold."

Controlling her shaking fingers as much as she could, given the view before her, Lou relayed the information to the emergency dispatcher. Once she'd given them all the information she could, Lou ended the call and stepped closer to Noah. The sound of sirens sliced through the night, cutting like an icy knife through the already frigid air.

Her gaze sweeping over the area, Lou's detail-oriented mind—that used to zero in on grammar, punctuation, and syntax errors back in her time as an editor—latched on to the minutiae of the scene. The handkerchief was white, but a pink stain covered more than half of it. The pink didn't seem to be related to the message scrawled upon the handkerchief in red marker, since the letters weren't bleeding or seeping down the fabric, proving whatever had stained the handkerchief had dried completely before the message had been written. There was a small red rose embroidered in the bottom left corner, and a hummingbird in the top right.

The handgun sat in Godfrey's lap, his fingers curled loosely around it, as if he'd been the one to hold it. But from the chair toppled on its side and the potted plant that was knocked over, it was clear there had been a struggle. Someone had likely placed that handkerchief over his face after he'd died.

Clues memorized, Lou asked, "How are we going to explain being here together?"

Noah squeezed his eyes together for a moment as he thought. "You're right. It's going to seem suspicious."

The word suspicious had a whole different meaning when they were standing in the presence of a body, but Lou knew Noah wasn't worried about them being suspects. He merely meant that people would ask questions about why they were alone in the woods together.

"We could use this as our reason to let the town know," Lou suggested. The timing wasn't perfect, but maybe it would have to do.

But Noah swung his head from side to side. "I'd really like to talk to Cassidy first."

Lou understood. She backed away. "What if I wasn't with you? What if I was at Willow's and I heard the sirens, so I came over to see what was wrong?" She took yet another step back toward the woods.

"That could work." Noah's eyes lit up in the intense flood of light from the Cranes' deck. His excitement turned into a frown, an expression that was even more pronounced in the contrasting lighting. "The nine-one-one dispatcher heard your voice, though."

She twitched a shoulder. "So? They're in the Lakeside county headquarters' building in Kirk. No one around here will know. The only person they might tell is Easton, and he already knows I was with you."

Noah's head began bobbing faster and faster. "Okay, yeah. Go back to Willow's and come back with her as if you're just curious. I think that'll work."

Sending him one last glance of support, Lou turned and ran through the woods, back toward Willow's. The sounds of the first emergency vehicle whizzed past, so by the time she reached Thread Lane, she crossed without worrying about any cars seeing her flee the scene. Willow was already on her porch, craning her neck to see what all the commotion was as Lou ran up to her house. Lou noted that Easton's car was still there.

"Easton?" Lou panted out the question between breaths. It hadn't been too far to run, but the cold air stung her lungs.

Willow jerked her thumb toward the Forest Park neighborhood. "He just took off on foot. I'm surprised you didn't pass him." Worry etched itself into a crease at the corner of her mouth. "What's going on? I couldn't get anything out of him before he left." While there was a hint of concern in Lou's best friend's voice, she didn't seem to be worried that anything had happened to Noah or anyone else they loved. Willow knew Lou would never have left if that were the case.

"Godfrey Crane was dead in his backyard. Shot." Lou finally caught her breath, though each exhale still created a billow of condensation as the warm air puffed out and mixed with the frosty air.

"And you're here because..." Willow looked her friend up and down.

"We didn't want to have to explain why we were together in the woods at night, so if anyone except for Easton asks, Noah found Godfrey on his own." Lou leveled her friend with a serious stare.

But she needn't worry. Willow lifted her chin in understanding and wrapped her coat tighter around her body. "Well, we'd better walk over there, then. Easton's going to want to know what you noticed."

Lou mentally checked the list she'd made while at the scene, making sure she remembered it all. It was likely Easton would notice everything as well, but he might ask her just in case.

She and Willow jogged across the street, coming at the Cranes' house from the front, like many of the others in the neighborhood. The construction crew working on the mansion had gone home for the night, and the giant building loomed ominously in the dark.

Shivering, Lou pulled her sleeves down to cover her fingers and then stuffed them into her pockets as they approached the scene. While the EMTs had arrived first, members from the police department were pulling up as Lou and Willow slowed. Officer Brennan, easily identifiable in his cruiser marked with the *K-9 Unit* decal on the side, parked in the driveway. He got out, joined by his partner,

Officer Peanut Butter. The bloodhound-Lab mix had helped solve a case last Christmas, and Lou hoped the dog would be just as helpful in this one.

Immediately, the dog's nose was to the ground as he took in every smell he could. Officer Brennan clicked his tongue, telling Peanut Butter it wasn't quite time to sniff yet, and he led the dog around to the backyard.

Keeping their distance, Lou and Willow watched as more police arrived, assisting with setting a perimeter around the area and taking statements from those who'd gathered.

"A gunshot has to be something the neighbors heard, right?" Willow whispered as she eyed the Lofall sisters who lived next door, and the Farmers, one house past that.

Lou agreed, but the question caused her lips to turn down. "Noah said the body felt cold. If it didn't just happen, why were we the first ones to call it in?" she asked.

"I didn't hear anything, and today's Wednesday, so I was here all day," Willow said.

Wednesdays were one of Willow's days off from her nursery. While her business partner, Peggy Lee, usually worked behind the scenes on her farm, growing the plants they sold at Valley Nursery, she'd insisted that Willow take at least one day a week to relax and recuperate so she didn't burn herself out. Willow had chosen Wednesdays, and even though Lou often found her studying pricing lists and sales figures on those days, she usually spent them in her own garden with her pygmy goat, Steve, and riding her horse, OC.

"Come to think of it," Willow added. "I couldn't hear

anything but the construction in the mansion. I think they must've been putting in floors today because it was all buzz saws and nail guns."

Lou took in the movement of the crime scene team as they swept the house. She inhaled sharply. "Maybe the neighbors didn't call it in because the gunshot blended in with the sound of the construction."

"Or they all worked together to kill him," Willow offered flatly. When Lou shot a glare in her direction, the woman put up her hands. "Fine, your explanation is more believable. It's just … everyone around here hated that man."

Lou leveled a glare at the mansion to their right. "True. And none more at the moment than Brock Nolan."

Until a few months ago, the mansion had barely been visible through the overgrown expanse of trees and shrubs that surrounded the property. But the first thing Brock had done upon purchasing the place was to have a team of landscapers work their magic on the decades of wild growth. They'd pruned, mowed, planted, and sometimes removed plants completely, until the result was something the people of Button might see in a home and garden magazine—well, all except the dilapidated house. But Brock had gotten to work on that next.

As far as he could, that is, until Godfrey had made it his mission to stop the progress on the mansion by calling in to the county to report the site any chance he could get.

Willow studied Lou, her surprised exhale billowing between them in a swirling cloud. "You think Brock might've done this?"

"Don't act so surprised," Lou whispered as the neighbors moved closer, as if they might come over to talk. "You're the one who mentioned Godfrey's neighbors as suspects, and Brock's his newest neighbor." She jabbed her thumb toward the mansion across the street.

Inclining her head in concession, Willow said, "Fine. I did. I just … Brock seems so unbothered by Godfrey, like the man isn't worth his time."

"Everyone has their breaking point, especially if Godfrey threatened him with that gun of his," Lou said, and they cut their conversation short, seeing the group of neighbors had wandered all the way over.

They all had the same stance: arms crossed, spines rigid, and shoulders hunched slightly forward to show the discomfort they all felt. Lou wondered where Cricket was, knowing the woman was too nosy to stay away, especially given all the cops swarmed around her backyard neighbor's house.

"That can't be good, can it?" Harmony Lofall gestured to the crime scene tape the officers had strung to prevent anyone from walking into the backyard.

Her sister, Mariah, winced and said, "Diana's out of town this week, so it has to be Godfrey."

Lou stiffened. She hadn't even considered his wife. The shock of finding him there on the deck had clouded everything else, and she'd completely forgotten that he'd been married for the better part of the year.

Godfrey and Diana had been a bit of a scandal last summer. It had been Lou's first summer in town, so she hadn't gotten involved in the gossip, but the locals were surprised, to say the least. Diana, the owner of the Bean and Button coffee shop, had come back from her yearly vacation to Vegas married, and to Godfrey Crane, owner of Crane Exteriors, a local house-painting business. Apparently, they'd both vacationed there, had run into one another by accident, and had hit it off. While the two remained sole owners of their businesses, they'd both spent that spring transitioning into more of a silent role to ready themselves for retirement, and could sympathize with the growing pains of such a decision.

As a frequent customer at the Bean and Button, Lou hadn't known the difference. Ruby, the manager of the coffee shop, was the only authority figure she knew.

"Does anyone know where Diana went?" Lou asked.

"Vegas," Mariah whispered, letting the destination hang in the air like she knew how much that one word said about the state of the couple's marriage.

She'd gone without him? To the place they'd tied the knot just over a year earlier? Lou's thoughts sent up red flags and warning bells.

Harmony sucked in a breath through clenched teeth. "I want to know what happened," she said, her voice strained with frustration.

"I don't," Lou said. It wasn't *really* a lie. She wished she didn't know, that she hadn't seen his body.

At least she didn't have to explain why. The crime scene tape kept everyone from guessing whether or not the man had died of natural causes.

"Yeah, but you don't live next door." Mariah shuddered, and the Farmers nodded in agreement. "And to think we were blissfully unaware, binging the newest season of Married to a Stranger all afternoon."

At her sister's mention of the television show, Harmony's shoulders scrunched up almost to her ears. "Anyone else here watch that show? Mariah and I are *obsessed*." She assessed the crowd but found they were all shaking their heads. That didn't seem to deter her. "They meet their spouse at the altar, and it's a genuine marriage. I just love it when it actually works out and they fall in love." She clapped her hands.

Just then, Noah rounded the back corner of the house, saving them from having to hear any more about the show.

"Noah?" Willow gasped his name in a such a dramatic fashion, Lou hoped she was the only one who caught that it was fake. "What are you doing here?"

Noah's gaze flicked to Lou's for a split second, as if he were checking to make sure she was okay. "Uh, I found him." He jabbed a thumb over his shoulder. "I was walking along the path to the pond and I..." Noah's throat bobbed with a heavy swallow.

"Why?" Joy Farmer's high-pitched voice cut through the night air like a knife, making Lou glad that the woman had kept quiet until then. "No one takes the northern path."

Based on the graying state of the woman's brown hair and the way her eyes narrowed, Joy had been living in that house long enough to remember when teenagers had used it as a date location like Noah had mentioned. The older woman scowled at Noah as if he were one of those very high schoolers, making out in the forest behind her house. Her quiet husband, Joe, mirrored her suspicious expression.

Panic moved thorough Lou, acting as an instant source of heat as her body flushed with worried thoughts. They hadn't planned out that part. They'd realized what a difficult position it would put them in if the town knew they'd been there together, alone, but hadn't ever come up with a reason for Noah to be there. Willow must've realized the same thing, because she discreetly grabbed on to Lou's hand with her own and squeezed tight.

Luckily, the man was smart as a whip, and he'd obviously thought about it. "Someone left an anonymous message at the clinic telling us they'd seen a hurt dog wandering the woods in this area. I came to check it out."

"In the dark?" Joy Farmer wasn't giving up.

Noah gave a clipped nod. "It's cold enough that I was worried about the animal staying out all night. But I didn't see anything. I hope it was just a prank. Sometimes we get those."

Joy huffed, but the discontented sound seemed directed at the idea of a prank instead of Noah. Lou breathed easier, and Willow lessened her death grip on Lou's fingers.

"Well"—Noah ran a hand over the back of his neck—"Willow and Lou, do you want me to walk back with you? I'm parked at Easton's."

"Sure." Willow waved at the Lofalls and the Farmers as she pivoted away, hooking her arm in Lou's as if she might not come willingly. But Lou was more than ready to get out of there.

"Did Easton want Lou's eyes on the scene?" Willow asked once they were far enough away from the group they'd just left, veering to the right as if they might cut through the woods and come at the house from behind to slip past the neighbors.

But Noah said, "I don't think so. It's pretty clear what happened. It was Godfrey's own gun in his lap, so he must've had it out to threaten someone who came to talk to him."

Brock? Lou wondered, not sure she wanted her initial guess to be correct. Brock Nolan was a transplant from Seattle and had recently purchased the old Rossback mansion, intent upon turning it from an eyesore to his dream house. He was quiet, but every interaction Lou'd had with the man had been positive, and she hated to think their newest resident would be capable of murder, even if he was pushed by a gun-toting, threatening Godfrey.

"I guess that's not a surprise." Willow snorted.

The whole town had heard the stories about showing up to Godfrey Crane's house to talk to him about something innocent and being met with his handgun held at his side like a threat. Apparently, he'd eased up on the paranoid behavior ever since Diana had moved in with him, but the compulsion to answer the door with his gun obviously hadn't gone away completely.

Or, Lou thought to herself, *he'd regressed into old habits lately, ever since things between him and Diana had started to go south.* It would make sense if Diana's solo trip was anything to go on.

"And the handkerchief?" Lou asked, turning her attention back to Noah as they walked up Easton and Willow's shared driveway. "It was covering his face and had the words *Stop the Vote* written on it in red marker," she told Willow.

"Yeah, Easton thinks it has to do with the Button Beautification Society and the vote on the proposition." Noah shrugged, as if that were pretty obvious too. "Brenner had Peanut Butter smell it, and they're going to have him present during their interrogations to see if he can catch the killer's scent."

Lou sighed as they reached the point in the driveway where it forked off to the two different houses, to where her car was parked at Willow's and Noah's truck was at Easton's. It sounded like Easton had seen everything she had.

"Sorry this ruined your night together," Willow said, the wrinkle in her nose just visible in the moonlight. "Do you want me to go inside so you can stare longingly into each other's eyes in the driveway?" She chuckled.

But the two of them couldn't seem to laugh as they looked across the road at the commotion in the Forest Pond neighborhood.

"That's okay," Lou said. "I might head home." Her eyes met Noah's in the darkness.

He bowed his head in understanding. Then, as if he could read the worried inner monologue running through her mind, he said, "Easton is the only one at the scene who knows you were with me. He said he'll come see you if he has questions. But he seemed confident they could close this quickly without trouble."

Lou hoped that would be the case.

CHAPTER 3

T he events of the evening had created such tunnel vision out of Lou's thoughts that she blinked in confusion as she walked through the back door into the bookstore and found the lights on. At first, she worried she'd left them on when she'd gone to meet Noah, but then she heard voices in the shop.

Walking forward instead of going up the stairs, Lou found George and Cricket sitting at the table by the front windows. Packaging for a cell phone sat between them, and George had the phone screen facing Cricket as she explained how to find the photos that had been transferred to the new device from her old one.

Right, Lou remembered. Not only was George staying with her, but she'd mentioned that Cricket might stop by later. That was probably why they hadn't seen her crowded in the neighborhood with the rest of the Forest Pond folks.

Gerald, George's cat, lay between the two—amid the box, charging cord, and user manual—proving he really couldn't bear to be more than a few feet away from George if he could help it. Sitting in the middle of the table probably made him feel like the center of attention instead of the phone. Meatball, an adorable tortoiseshell and Lou's newest foster, was draped over Cricket's lap, sleeping contentedly.

"Hey," George said as she glanced over her shoulder at Lou. "How was Willow?"

Swallowing, Lou couldn't seem to find her voice. She stammered for a moment before blurting out, "Someone shot Godfrey Crane."

George's eyelids fluttered. "He's … dead?"

Lou let her head dip forward, and pulled it back upright, but the motion took considerable effort. It all felt surreal. George seemed to agree. Her cheeks puffed out, and she released an exhale from her lips like air leaking out of a balloon.

Cricket, on the other hand, scoffed and pretended to spit over her left shoulder. "Good riddance, I say."

George's eyes practically doubled in size.

"Cricket!" Lou couldn't believe the woman.

Their reactions didn't seem to affect her, though, and she straightened in her seat. "I will not apologize for being honest about that terrible man. He made everyone in that neighborhood suffer for decades, and that wasn't enough for him. That inane proposition of his would've allowed him to terrorize the whole town if it went far enough to become a new ordinance."

Lou's mind returned to the handkerchief and the note that had been written on it before it had been placed on his face.

"Wait. I haven't heard about a new ordinance. What was happening?" George squinted one eye.

Cricket's mouth parted in shock. "Where have you been living? Under a rock?"

"No," George answered flatly. "But I have been dealing with a termite infestation, coordinating with the flooring people to get to work once the tenting is done, moving my life over here, and trying to keep my business running through all of it. Sorry if I missed a tiny bit of town drama in the process."

"Well, first of all, it's not a tiny bit of drama," Cricket said with a snort. "It's the very principle of individuality on the line. The man created a group called the Button Beautification Society, or the BBS for short, with the sole goal of voting in a new town ordinance that would ensure all businesses and residences within town limits fit within the sewing theme of our streets."

George's nostrils flared as if she smelled something bad. "The BBS? Really? Did no one learn from the *BSB*?"

As someone who'd been more involved than she'd wanted to be with the *Behind the Scenes in Button*, or *BSB*, blogger a few months ago, Lou shared George's sentiment.

Moving past that, George asked, "What would that entail? Fitting into the sewing theme?"

Lou could answer that question. "The society argued that our tourism rates, while good, could improve if we became one of those themed towns where everything has to be approved by the zoning board to make sure it fits with the agreed-upon aesthetic. They want all houses to be one of a dozen preapproved colors, all businesses to have sewing-themed names, the streetlights to be painted to look like needles, planters like spools … stuff like that." Lou couldn't seem to remember everything that had been listed on the proposition they'd presented to the town council at the last meeting. "Basically, it would be a Homeowners Association for the whole town."

"And it would mean the end of individuality, not to mention thousands of dollars out of the pocket of every resident, more for businesses needing to change their names." Cricket shook her head. "All because he wanted a reason to block that Brock Nolan from the construction he's doing at the mansion out there across from Godfrey's home."

"You really think he started the BBS just to stop Brock?" Lou asked, considering how quickly her mind had jumped to Brock as a suspect as well.

Cricket's shoulder blades drew together, straightening her posture. "Either that, or he did it to line his pockets. Who do you think would be hired to paint the majority of houses in town if everyone was forced to change their house colors?"

"Crane Exteriors," Lou whispered. And even though Godfrey Crane wasn't part of the day-to-day operations anymore, the man would most definitely benefit financially from such a surge in business.

"Maybe both factored into his reasoning," Cricket added.

A deep crease formed in George's forehead. "You keep saying him, but it sounds like there was an entire group fighting for this. Why would someone kill just Godfrey?"

"Well"—Cricket leaned forward—"It's my suspicion that the rest of the group was just with him because the zoning laws would make it easier to keep out big business-es." Cricket rolled her eyes. "It's the same players who've been telling us for years that the big chains are trying to come in and take over our town." Cricket peered over each shoulder. "But, surprise, I don't see that happening. They freak out over nothing. The BBS may be new but those same individuals have been fighting to keep things from changing in Button for years, individually. They've gotten further with Godfrey at the helm than they ever have alone, but he was the only one who cared about the town theme."

George squeezed her eyes shut for a moment, like she was trying to digest all the information. "Wait, and why doesn't Godfrey want Brock to restore the old Rossback mansion? Isn't it better for everyone if that place is fixed up?"

Cricket let out a long swoosh of air. "Who knows? The reason he gave each time he called to complain about the work or call a permit into question was safety. In reality, it probably had something to do with his property taxes going—"

But Cricket didn't have time to finish that statement, because her new phone began ringing from where it sat on the table. The sound startled Geralt awake, and he stared at the thing. The fear in his eyes was mirrored in Cricket's, and she seemed equally frozen in place.

"Aren't you going to answer it?" George asked, pointing to the thing as it trilled out a terribly loud retro phone-ringing sound.

"Right." Cricket swallowed and picked it up. She poked at the screen and then held it tentatively to her ear. "This is Cricket." Eyebrows jumping, she said, "Oh, hi, Easton. Sorry, I'm actually at the bookshop. Yes, with Lou." There was another pause. "Sure. You can come here." At that comment, Cricket glanced up at Lou, who nodded that it was okay. "See you soon." She ended the call.

"What was that about?" George leaned closer.

"He needs to ask me some questions," she said nonchalantly, as if she was sure it was about nothing more scandalous than one of her embroidery classes. But her gaze flicked up to meet Lou's and then back at the phone, making Lou realize that indifference had been forced.

Was Cricket worried about Easton asking her questions about Godfrey's death? Lou kept the thoughts to herself. The woman had been outspoken against the man and had made some threatening remarks earlier that day.

An unmarked cruiser pulled up in front of the bookstore and the tall detective stepped out. Lou met Easton at the front door, unlocking it for him. He greeted her and then the two women at the table as he stepped inside.

As if sensing a man had entered, Meatball jumped off Cricket's lap and rushed toward the safety of the bookshelves. Not holding the same fear of men as the tortoiseshell, Geralt stayed put, eyeing the detective.

"Sorry to bother you," Easton said to no one in particular. He wasn't wearing his normal suit, but had on jeans and a hooded sweatshirt instead, proving he must've been hanging out with Willow when he'd gotten the call about Godfrey. "Cricket, do you want to step into Lou's office to talk?" He glanced up at Lou in question, asking if that was okay.

About to nod in concession that it was fine, Lou was interrupted by Cricket saying, "Whatever you have to ask me, you can ask it in front of these two." Despite the dismissive nature of her words, the older woman's voice trembled. She gripped her phone tighter, as if trying to calm shaking fingers.

Easton only hesitated for a beat before he pulled out the last chair at the table. He slid a notepad from his jacket and set it in front of him. His fingers fished around in the same pocket until he produced a pen.

"Okay, Cricket, I need to know what you were doing between the hours of eleven and three this afternoon." Easton's grayish-blue eyes locked on to the older woman, studying her reaction to the request.

But instead of continuing to grow agitated, Cricket's chest expanded as she pulled in a deep breath and then let it go in relief. "I was at the quilt shop." She lifted her chin. "I taught an embroidery class from eleven to twelve, then I worked at the cutting counter to help Rosa until she closed up at five. I went home to find my new phone had arrived in the mail. So, after having dinner with Peter, I came over to get George's help with setting it up."

Easton scribbled out notes as she spoke. Before he could ask a question, Cricket tapped on the table.

"Rosa was there the whole time. She can vouch for me. So can my students." After Noah's mother's name, Cricket listed off the names of five locals who'd been in her class.

What felt like the weight of a brick lifted from Lou's

chest. She breathed easily as Cricket's solid alibi cleared the anxiety that had been blocking her airway. But the relief was short-lived because, if Cricket hadn't been the one to hurt Godfrey, why had she acted so nervous about the possibility of being questioned by Easton?

Easton nodded, as if punctuating the end to his questioning. He pointed his pen at Cricket. "You're lucky you have an alibi, especially after all the threats you've made toward the man lately."

"Believe me. I know it." The woman placed a hand on her chest. "I'm upset that I put myself in this situation."

That seemed to be enough for Easton. He stood, said his goodbyes, and returned to his cruiser. Lou hoped he would be able to get some sleep that night. But with Detective Anderson's departure a couple of months earlier, Easton was the only detective left in town. Officer Brenner had stepped up quite a bit, but he was still fairly new to the force.

Once Lou had relocked the door behind Easton, she turned back to Cricket and George. Hand on her hip, Lou leveled the older woman with a glare. "Okay, what was that all about?"

Cricket motioned toward the street. "Easton? He was asking—"

"No," Lou interrupted her. "I know what Easton was doing. I want to know why you were so flustered by it. If you have an alibi, why did you seem like you'd been caught?"

Any bravado left Cricket in a hissed-out breath. She let her head hang forward. "Because I was."

George and Lou shared a worried glance but kept quiet as they turned their attention back to Cricket. Still, Lou's pulse thumped as they waited. Was Cricket about to tell them that she'd lied to the detective?

"I ran my mouth, and if I hadn't had a good alibi, I could very well be one of the main suspects on that list Easton's making right now." She held her arm out toward the police station. A shiver worried up her back. She shook her shoulders. "I'm lucky, but it still unsettled me."

That made sense. Lou had been falsely accused before, and it had been far from pleasant.

Drumming her fingers on her phone, Cricket said, "Well, I'd better get home to Peter. He's probably all in a tizzy about the police presence at the Cranes'." She stood and patted George's shoulder. "Thank you for the tech assist, dear."

"Anytime, Cricket. Have a good night." George placed the manual and cord back into the box and handed it over to the older woman.

Lou hugged the woman before letting her out the door just as she had with Easton minutes earlier. She and George exhaled in tandem once they were alone.

"At least we don't have to deal with someone we love being accused of murder, again," George said. She hoisted Geralt up off the table and started for the stairs.

Following, Lou turned off the bookshop lights. But even as she agreed, Lou couldn't help the foreboding feeling that sat in her gut at the thought that it might not be that easy.

CHAPTER 4

Having George staying in the guest bedroom reminded Lou of when her nieces had visited her the summer before. Even though George was in her twenties, instead of in her teens like Maddy and Mia, she still brought a youthful spirit to Lou's home.

While Lou and George had become fast friends the first day Lou had moved to town, they were very different people.

George turned up her nose at Lou's offer to make extra coffee the next morning, while Lou sneered at the energy drink George downed instead. Lou tended to listen to an audiobook or a podcast while she got ready for work, but George played loud music that leaked through the bathroom walls.

Lou stuck earbuds in and finished her podcast while she made herself breakfast, setting a second serving of scrambled eggs and toast aside for George in case she was hungry. Breakfast seemed to be where they agreed, and they ate in companionable silence.

"What's your schedule like today?" Lou asked, minding the small herd of cats that wound through their legs and around their feet as they descended the back staircase into the bookshop a short while later.

George was not just the person everyone in Button went to when they needed a new technological device. She was also the unofficial tech support for the community—most of which fit squarely in that "technologically uncomfortable" category. At her home, she normally just let folks filter in throughout the day as they clutched whichever device was giving them problems. A note on the door with a loose timeline for when she would return usually sufficed if she needed to leave, but Lou didn't know if George would be more or less structured in her temporary space.

George adjusted Geralt in his baby wrap, and the cat purred even louder in response, obviously happy with the way she'd tucked his foot into the carrier. "Mrs. Green said she's having trouble with her tablet, so she's going to bring that in around lunchtime, and Boyd wants to buy one of the video doorbells for his shop, so I'm going to talk him through the options. He said he'd be in this morning, but the man is notoriously late, so I'm not going to hold my breath." She chuckled. "Other than that, I can help around the shop."

They stepped into the bookshop, and Lou felt the usual happy tug at her heart, the one that told her she was in the exact place she was supposed to be, doing exactly what she was meant to.

"Don't feel obligated, though," Lou reminded George. "I know you've got your own business to run, and we can easily coexist in this space. In fact"—she gestured to the table at the front of the shop—"why don't you commandeer that table for your Tech Emporium needs for the length of your stay."

A warm smile spread across George's face. "I appreciate it. Thank you. But I also don't mind helping with the bookshop. If you want to leave at all, just say the word. I'll watch over everything for you."

Thanking her, Lou couldn't foresee needing to leave, but it was nice to have the option. Most of the time, her need to leave the shop coincided with solving some mystery or another around town. But with Cricket being cleared as a suspect because of her alibi, no one Lou knew and loved was involved in Godfrey's murder, and she didn't foresee needing to get involved in the case.

That conviction lessened later that morning when her busy bookshop became downright crowded when Easton entered, followed by a gaggle of locals yapping at the detective's back. Easton pinched the bridge of his nose before turning to address them.

"I told you, he's not a suspect," Easton said. Based on the mixture of fatigue and frustration backing the sentence, Lou guessed it wasn't the first time he'd said it that morning.

A man named Fred snorted. "Sure, so you expect us to believe that he just happened to be walking by?"

Easton nodded in one long, fatigued movement. "I really do, Fred."

"What about Tammy seeing him walking toward Forest Pond earlier in the day, when Godfrey was actually shot?" a woman named Ria asked, pointing over to where the aforementioned Tammy stood, arms crossed like a child who'd been too easily dismissed.

Nostrils flaring as he inhaled what seemed like sanity-saving breath, Easton said, "Walking in the same direction as the Cranes' house does not make him guilty of Godfrey's murder."

Lou's ears perked up at the conversation. Did this small mob have a suspect in mind? She and Willow had conjectured Brock Nolan had the best motive to kill the leader of the Button Beautification Society. Had someone seen him walking toward the Crane household the day of the crime?"

Easton strode over to where Lou stood behind the checkout counter and leaned closer to her. Whispering so the gathering crowd couldn't hear him, Easton leaned forward and said, "I really wish the two of you didn't want to keep your relationship a secret. It would be a lot easier to tell them you were with Noah when he found the body."

The comment felt like icy fingers around her heart. They thought *Noah* had something to do with Godfrey Crane's death? The person they suspected wasn't Brock Nolan, but Noah Ramero? The thought took a moment to take seed in Lou's mind. It felt so out of the realm of possibility.

"Yeah," Fred added. "Do we really believe this *story* about him searching for a stray in the woods? No one around that area had heard of one, and he didn't end up finding anything … well … anything but Godfrey."

"Just like he'd planned," Ria said, stretching out the

words conspiratorially. Her cheeks flushed pink as she took in Lou's probably aghast expression, mistaking it for anger. "I mean, *maybe*. We don't know for sure." She shot an apologetic glance at Lou.

While the town might not know the truth about her romantic relationship with Noah, they were all well aware that the two of them were friends, and that Noah helped Lou with the rescue cats in the bookshop. They should've known better than to talk about him around her, or Easton, for that matter.

But whereas Ria had shown restraint, given her present company, Fred didn't seem to have any qualms about accusing Noah in front of his friends. "All I know is that Cricket is like a second mom to Noah. He'd do anything for her. And she suspiciously has an alibi for the window when Godfrey was shot."

"Suspicious?" Easton exhaled the word, the question in his tone pained. "She was working in the quilt shop, like she always does. How in the world is that suspicious?"

"Just a little too convenient, if you ask me." Fred tapped his bulbous nose.

"Well, no one did, Fred. That's the problem," Silas said from where he was trying, and failing, to read the news-paper on the love seat in the sitting area.

Fred's cheeks reddened, and he glared at the other crotchety old man. For her part, Lou felt grateful for her grumpy regular, especially when Fred muttered something about Easton playing favorites before he left the bookshop.

Without Fred there, Ria, Tammy, and the rest of them left as well. Lou was about to ask Easton to fill her in on everything that had happened leading up to that mob of misinformed followers, but Noah walked into the bookshop.

The dark circles under his eyes and the frown line between his eyebrows were all the signs of confirmation that Lou needed to prove that Easton wasn't the only one who'd been bombarded with questions surrounding Noah's whereabouts yesterday.

"George, could you watch the register for a moment?" Lou asked. When the young woman got up to trade places, Lou latched on to the nearest cat she could find. The closest one turned out to be Charles Lickens. Lou tucked the cat tight to her side. "Noah, I think there's something wrong with Charles's ears. Would you come back to the office with me to check them out?"

He didn't say anything, but tiredly followed her to the back office.

Lou locked the door behind them. She quickly put the cat down onto the floor. Noah seemed to understand that she'd made up the ear problem to get him back there, because he focused on her instead of Charles Lickens.

"I'm guessing you've heard?" She swallowed as she waited for his answer.

Noah's eyes closed in a lengthy blink, the motion taking so long it seemed like he was moving underwater, like he didn't have the strength to go faster. "You mean, have I heard that a large portion of the town worries I was the one to turn Godfrey's gun on him and shoot him?" He grunted out a humorless laugh. "Yeah, I heard something of the sort."

Lou slid her hands through the spaces created between his arms and torso. She snaked her arms up his back, pulling him close to her. "I'm so sorry. It's all because we said you were alone. If they knew I was there, they wouldn't be questioning you. I didn't even think this would be a problem."

"Don't put this on you, or us." Noah snorted. "This isn't because of us having to pretend you weren't there. Regardless of whether I'd been the one to find Godfrey, half the town seems to think I'd do anything Cricket told me, even get rid of someone she'd hated and threatened."

"They said you were walking toward the Cranes' house around the time Godfrey was shot," Lou repeated what she'd heard Fred say.

Noah groaned. "Yes, Cricket asked me to grab her lunch from her house because she'd forgotten it and was teaching. I picked it up and left, heading back for the quilt shop." He released a tight breath. "The facts don't matter to them, and neither will this wild theory they've pieced together, not in a day or two. It'll be fine."

Lou looked up into his face, her hand moving up with her gaze to cup his cheek. "It doesn't seem fine. It seems like it has upset you."

Breath rushed out of him with a grunt. Noah let his head tilt toward her hand, resting some of the weight of it in her palm.

"I wish they thought better of me. They know me." The lines of his throat tightened. "It stings a little to know that they could think of me in such a terrible light." Shrugging off the truth behind his feelings, Noah said, "But as I said, it'll pass. They'll find someone else who was walking their dog at the time, who will have a different circumstantial reason to be considered a suspect, and they'll move on."

Lou hoped the man was right. But as she observed the negative way it was affecting him to think of his friends and neighbors believing such an awful thing about him, she doubted his words. The case had already proved to be more complicated than she first thought. And she had a feeling they weren't done getting thrown curveballs.

CHAPTER 5

After the tension sitting over the downtown area like a weighted blanket Thursday, Friday came in like a gust of crisp, fall air. Noah, it seemed, had been absolutely correct. By Friday, Brock Nolan was the new talk of the town as word spread about Godfrey's attempts to stop the construction of Brock's mansion, and the way the man had ignored the requests.

"Keeping those loud crews working would've been a great way to cover the sound of the gunshot," the locals conjectured.

"But how could he have predicted Godfrey would answer the door with his gun?" another person asked.

"When doesn't Godfrey answer the door with that gun?" someone else added. "I bet Brock stirred him up, then went over there to 'talk' and turned that gun on him once he invited him inside." That was just one theory, though all seemed to have Brock as the prime suspect.

Unlike when they'd pointed fingers at Noah, this time

Easton agreed with everyone, because he brought Brock Nolan in for questioning Friday around lunchtime.

It hadn't helped the man's innocence that he'd been unreachable for the day following the murder of Godfrey Crane. And while Brock assured the town he'd been gathering more supplies up north for the mansion renovation, the townspeople muttered about how there was still cell service up north, and that it shouldn't have taken him so long to get back to the detective, and return to town.

"Mariah Lofall said Brock stormed over to the Crane residence that morning. He was red faced and had his fingers all balled into a fist like he might punch Godfrey," one Buttonite relayed as the conversation in the bookshop turned to Brock's obvious guilt.

As much as Lou didn't love them making the same leaps in judgment as they had with Noah, her relief that their interest had moved on to someone else won out. It also didn't hurt that she'd had the same questions about Brock when she'd first realized Godfrey was dead.

Staying focused on the conversation at hand, another local added, "Sasha said Brock was still there yelling when she arrived for the BBS meeting."

The name rang a bell with Lou. Sasha Richards was the owner of Slice of Button, the local pizza parlor, and a member of the Button Beautification Society. As the locals gossiped, it seemed more and more likely that Brock had finally cracked under Godfrey's attempts to thwart his renovation and must've been the one to confront Godfrey. Lou had sympathy for how difficult Godfrey had made Brock's life ever since he'd started the renovations on the mansion across the street, but she had no pity for someone who solved problems with violence, especially murder.

She hadn't heard from Noah all morning, so she sent him a text around lunchtime.

Sounds like you were right. All anyone can talk about is Brock.

When she didn't hear back right away, Lou tucked her phone into the top drawer of the checkout counter and worked on straightening the shelves. Putting books back in their correct places and filling holes left by customers buying books was a constant job, one Lou loved. The absolute satisfaction she felt when a row of shelves was back to its fully stocked, pristine state made a warmth rush up from her toes as if she were standing directly in front of the cast-iron stove in the corner of the bookshop.

Speaking of the stove, she added another log to the fire. While she'd yet to step foot outside that day, her customers had all come in shivering and complaining of the biting early November wind. The cats all lounged within a yard or two of the fireplace.

Sapphire, Lou's white cat, was the farthest away, choosing to sleep on a fleece cat bed on one of the lower bookshelves nearby in a blank space Lou left throughout the shelves for the cats. Charles Lickens and Anne Mice were both stretched out on the ground before the hearth. When Lou had first opened the shop, she'd been worried customers might step on the cats when they lay like that. But her sign on the front door warning people that there were multiple cats inside, and they should watch their step, seemed to do the job because they'd never had an incident.

Meatball was perched on the windowsill, opening her eyes every once in a while to "hunt" the crisp fall leaves that blew down the street. George had left Geralt upstairs since, if he wasn't attached to his owner's body, he had the terrifying tendency to throw himself in front of people's feet as they walked, hoping for attention. It was safer for everyone if he remained up there.

The bell on the front door chimed, interrupting Lou's thoughts about the cats. She turned around to find Noah entering the bookshop, carrying a brown bag she recognized as takeout from the bistro down the street.

Noah's dark brown eyes locked on to Lou for a moment before he scanned the rest of the shop, searching for customers. Lou shook her head, letting him know there wasn't anyone else there at the moment. It was just them.

"George went to the Burnsides to help them with an internet-router issue," Lou explained. "And I haven't seen any of the regulars today."

"They're probably all having pizza for lunch, would be my guess." Noah cocked an eyebrow.

The Slice of Button building was right next door to the police station, and the tables in the front windows had an especially good view of the front door and parking lot of the Button Police Department.

"Not you, though." Lou's lip curved up on one side as she motioned to the bag he held.

He matched her half smile with one of his own, the movement bringing out the dimple in that cheek. "Us. I brought you lunch." Wetting his lips, he asked, "You didn't get my texts?"

Eyes flashing wide, Lou glanced over at the checkout counter where she'd stashed her phone. She hadn't checked it since she'd sent him that text, having lost track of time with her organizing.

"Sorry," she said, cringing.

Noah's shoulders bobbed as he brushed it off. "I got your favorite."

Lou's heart melted at his thoughtfulness. She gestured to the table in between them, quickly moving books she'd put there for a customer to look through earlier. Noah's brow creased for a moment as he set down the bag because Sapphire wasn't sleeping in his usual spot on the other pile of books on the table. His gaze wandered through the shop until he found the white cat sleeping on a shelf nearby.

As happy as Lou was to have Noah there with her for lunch, her gaze flicked up to him a few times as he pulled the food from the bag.

"What?" He chuckled. "Why do you keep staring at me like that?"

Lou cut her eyes to the window. "Are you sure we should be having lunch like this? Anyone walking past can see us."

And they *would* peer in. It had taken Lou time to get used to life in a small town. People would actually stop and look in windows. Luckily, they seemed to draw the line at businesses and weren't going around spying on people inside their houses. But Lou still found it unsettling after living in New York City, where people minded their own business.

With the gray clouds covering the sky and the warm, orangey glow of the lights in the bookshop, passersby wouldn't even need to cup their hands on the windows. They'd be able to see directly inside, almost as if it were night.

"I could close the shop for a bit, and we could go upstairs to eat." Lou took the fork Noah handed her from the bag, but jabbed it up toward her apartment, where they wouldn't be on display.

"What?" Noah gave her a sly smile. "We had plenty of meals together when we were just friends. This isn't weird."

Lou pressed her lips together to keep herself from disagreeing with him. He was the one who had more to lose if word got out about them. If he was comfortable with them being seen having lunch together, then Lou supposed she was too.

She took a seat opposite Noah, and they peeled off the lids of the aluminum to-go containers. The cheesy, rich smell of Lou's favorite lasagna wafted up to greet her. She let out a hum of appreciation.

"Thank you. This is perfect." It was just the comfort food she longed for on bone-chilling days like this one.

Noah beamed, his eyes crinkling at the corners as he watched her. "I had a cancellation right before lunch." He speared a piece of pasta from the carbonara he'd ordered for himself. "So, speaking of people seeing us together, I was thinking a lot last night about telling Cassidy, and when would be the best time to do that."

Lou ate as she listened. She knew it was a delicate issue, especially since Cassidy knew Lou, and she'd become a big part of both the community and Marigold's life. And while Lou could easily picture what Marigold's reaction would eventually be to the news—the hugs would be so tight they might bruise—Lou couldn't seem to settle on what she thought Cassidy would say.

"Cass has a new client who's motivated to buy," Noah explained. "Which means she's going to be super focused on that until she gets them to sign a contract. You know what that's like."

Lou did. Both Noah and Marigold had mentioned her obsessive work habits before, but Lou had seen it firsthand during Cassidy's last sale. Noah had an emergency client and had asked if Lou could grab Marigold for him on their regular switch day. She hadn't hesitated, but when she'd gone to pick up the girl, Cassidy—normally put together and organized—had been almost manic and distracted. The sheer amount of overthinking Lou witnessed had been a surprise even though she'd already heard the stories.

"We can definitely wait until she has that off her plate." Lou sent Noah a reassuring smile.

It quickly dropped as the bookshop door swung open and George stepped inside. Her nose worked first as she sniffed the delicious smells coming from their lunch. But it was her eyes that next took in the scene in front of her. They narrowed as she looked from Lou to Noah, then back to Lou.

Worry crept down each of Lou's limbs, out to the tips of her fingers and toes.

"Heyyyy." George cocked her head to one side as she stepped closer to the table. "What's happening here?"

Lou inwardly cringed. It was obvious they were just having lunch, so the question was unmistakably about so much more than just the meal. Noah, whose back was still to George, flashed an apologetic, slightly panicky look at Lou.

She had to fix this.

Before Lou or Noah could answer, however, the door opened again, and in stepped Silas and Cricket together. Silas helped Cricket out of her heavy wool jacket before he took off his own, hanging them both on the coatrack Lou kept by the door.

They seemed to go through the same thought processes George had, if their flared nostrils, then questioning gazes were anything to go by.

"What's happening here?" Cricket repeated George's question from moments before. Her voice rose conspiratorially, leaving no question about what she *thought* was happening.

Lou's mind worked as quickly as it could. "Noah lost a bet," she said, not even leaving them enough time to ask questions before she added, "I told him that the town would forget about him being a suspect in Godfrey's murder within twenty-four hours. He bet me lunch they wouldn't." She stabbed the fork into the lasagna. "I won."

There. That sounded like friends. That was definitely

something they might've done before they'd started anything romantic.

Noah sent a covert wink at her. The group of regulars let out a series of groans and scoffs. As if they'd all been summoned there at once to ruin their meal, Forrest walked in at that very moment, just slightly behind the rest.

"What?" he asked, frowning as he took in their expressions.

Cricket waved a hand toward him. "We're just talking about how silly it is that the townspeople even mentioned Noah's name in connection with Godfrey's murder. But our Noah can't keep a secret to save his life. There's no way he had anything to do with this."

Lou and Noah shared an almost imperceptible smile, knowing he was keeping one pretty big secret, though it had nothing to do with Godfrey.

"*And* there's no way he could've hurt someone," George added slowly, like the woman had lost it.

"Right." Cricket lifted one shoulder. "So, anyway, who's going to the meeting tonight?" She rubbed her hands together. "I made signs for anyone who'd like to hold one."

The town council meeting, Lou realized. With Godfrey's death, she'd forgotten that the very vote mentioned on that handkerchief covering his face was set to happen that evening.

The group of Lou's regulars continued the conversation about the meeting as they wandered over to the sitting area in the middle of the bookshop, leaving Lou and Noah to finish their lunch.

Lou took another bite of her lasagna and chanced a

glance at Noah. He looked up from where he was still eating his pasta, but the way his white teeth flashed as he swallowed a bite made Lou wish she could shove everyone out and lock the door behind them for some alone time.

"What do you want to bet that we won't have a choice in whether we hold one of those signs tonight?" Lou whispered.

Noah chuckled. "She can be very convincing." His grin faded. "Let's just hope it's enough."

Lou hoped it would be too. She hadn't hated Godfrey Crane as much as Cricket, but she also didn't want the town to turn into a place where businesses and people felt stifled by the rules and regulations.

"It'll be interesting. That's for sure." Lou crossed her fingers and mentally prepared herself for the meeting.

She didn't know what to expect, given that someone had already been killed over the subject. Lou could only hope violence wouldn't rear its head again in connection with the vote.

CHAPTER 6

That evening, Lou drove out to the community center, past Button Memorial Park, for the town council meeting. George, Cricket, and Noah had driven together, but Lou had a customer walk in just a few minutes before closing, so she'd told her friends to go on without her.

With how outspoken Cricket was about the whole situation, Lou wasn't exactly sad to arrive separately.

The community center held a distinct "old school" smell, probably because it used to be the elementary school building before the town got the funds to build the newer one up by the middle and high schools. Signs simple enough that they could've been created in Microsoft Word —printed out and taped onto the walls—directed Lou to the gym. The schedule on the wall outside the large room told Lou that in addition to being where they held town council meetings, they also held their youth basketball, recreational volleyball, and senior fitness classes.

Slipping in quietly through the doors at the back, Lou found the meeting had already started.

"If there are no more new items to add to the agenda, we can move on to the propositions from the different committees," Kyle Goldblume, the most senior town council member, said from the middle of the long table at the front.

The audience had separated themselves like families at a wedding. Both sections had signs, but Lou could tell right away that Cricket had made most of the ones for the opposition, given the sizable pile that still sat next to her seat along the right-hand side of the gym.

On Cricket's side, signs like *This is SEW wrong, Don't sew our mouths shut,* and *Let us keep our individuality* were being hoisted into the air. There were even a few that had *Stop the Vote* written on them, causing a shiver to curl up Lou's spine as she remembered the handkerchief the killer had placed over Godfrey's face. She hoped the people with those signs hadn't heard about it. If they had … well, it was too morbid to consider.

The right side overflowed from the seats, and while Lou found Cricket and George in the center of one of the rows, she noticed that Noah and some others had opted to stand against the wall to make room—and possibly to remove themselves from the loudest section of the group.

The side holding the Button Beautification Society and its supporters was considerably smaller, but they still packed most of the seats. Their signs were less colorful than the ones Cricket had made, holding sayings like, *Keep big business out of Button!*

At Kyle's mention of moving on to the propositions, the crowd grew louder. Lou found Silas standing near the back, a bag of potato chips tucked into the crook of his arm. She sidled over to him instead of trying to navigate the wild mess that was the opposing side.

Silas crunched on a chip as he raised his gray eyebrows at Lou in a greeting. He held the bag out toward her, but she shook her head, turning her attention back to the crowd.

"People, if you can't quiet down, we won't be able to go through with this vote," Kyle said, his voice thick with fatigue.

"Good," someone yelled from the opposition. "It should never have been allowed through in the first place."

The people sitting on the left side swiveled toward the speaker. But they didn't rebuke as Lou expected them to.

"Actually, Kyle, we would like to call for a delay in the vote on our town-theme proposition." A woman who appeared to be about Lou's age stood in the crowd. She had short, dark hair and kept her chin lifted as if she were trying to stay above the pettiness the opposing side emitted.

Kyle shielded his eyes from the lights at the front so he could see her more clearly. "Robin? Is that you?"

"Robin Granger," Silas muttered into Lou's ear. "She owns the storage facility out on Hem Avenue."

Lou nodded in understanding as Robin mirrored the gesture. "Yes, this request comes from me and the *remaining* BBS members."

The emphasis Robin put on that particular word told

Lou as much as she needed to know about where the woman was going with the request. The rest of the group stood facing the front. Lou recognized Sasha Richards from Slice of Button. The thirtysomething woman was a spitfire, and had made the local pizza spot a success because of her dedication to the combination of great crust, perfect sauce, and a fun environment. Moving down the row, Lou recognized Mitchell Moore, mostly because his house was kitty-corner from Willow's and Easton's homes on Pattern Drive. He was the oldest of their group. In fact, Lou could've sworn the man was retired. What was he doing in a group with local business owners? Next to Mitchell was a younger man Lou didn't recognize.

"Adam Stout," Silas said, following her squinty-eyed gaze. "Owns the grocery store. Well, his family does. He's poised to take over once his parents retire."

Adam and Sasha seemed to be about the same age. But Lou didn't discount them because of their youth. Not only had she seen Sasha's success, but George, who was even younger than both of them, ran one of the more successful businesses in Button.

Robin cleared her throat. "Seeing how one of our own was shot down for his beliefs less than two days ago, we need some time to mourn."

A heavy silence fell over the room.

For a moment. Then someone on the opposing side called out, "You're just using that as an excuse because you know you're going to lose the vote, and you want more time to bribe people into voting your way."

Silas coughed in surprise, covering his mouth so he

wouldn't spit chips everywhere. Swallowing, he leaned toward Lou and said, "Bold."

Lou had to agree.

Sasha Richards stood and sneered to the right, obviously not sure who'd said that. "Of course, we won't get the votes when your side is killing people to stop our proposition from moving on to the next step."

The room seemed to take a collective inhale.

Someone called out, "You think they killed Godfrey because of the vote?" Even though the voice sounded a lot like the last person who'd yelled, this question was quieter, humbled.

Snorting, Sasha said, "Of course we do."

"But ... I thought Brock killed him for stopping the work on his mansion," another person ventured, indignation raising their volume and tone.

"They let Brock go about an hour ago," someone called from the back.

Murmurs swept through the old gym.

"It's true. I talked to him," a person near the front called out. "He had an alibi. He was up in Bellingham, at that kitchen supply warehouse picking up his granite countertops, and he said there's no way he could've gotten back in time to kill Godfrey, so Easton had to let him go."

Gasps rose from the crowd, Lou's own among them. Silas almost choked on his chips again.

Sasha cut her glare over at Noah. "See? Even more proof that it was one of you."

Lou's heart ached for Noah as his jaw clenched in anger. She wanted so badly to step forward and come to his defense, to let everyone know she was with him. But Cricket stood, taking the pressure off Noah.

"Let them have their extension. They didn't have enough votes to push this through with Godfrey, and they're not going to the next time they try either." The older woman sniffed at the left side of the gym.

Sasha rolled her eyes, but sat as Kyle tapped his fingers against the microphone in his hand.

"Okay, it sounds like we're all in agreement that we should push this matter." He flipped through some papers in front of him. "If you're hoping to get it on the next ballot, however, the latest we can push the vote would be next week." Kyle glanced up. "Button Beautification Society, it's your call."

"Next week will be fine." Robin crossed her arms.

Kyle dipped his chin in acknowledgment. "Okay, everyone. We will reconvene next Friday, same place, same time." He winced. "Why don't we leave the signs at home next time? We're all neighbors. I'm sure we can handle this civilly."

A few scoffs rang out in the crowd as if they doubted that, but no one argued as Kyle ended the meeting. Just as people began standing from their seats, Easton sidled over to stand next to Lou and Silas.

"What'd I miss?" he whispered.

Lou's eyes widened at the sight of him. "The BBS called to postpone the vote until next week, since Godfrey was killed."

"And you were a topic of conversation, seeing as you let Brock go," Silas grumbled from the other side of Lou.

"How'd they kn—" Easton stopped himself. "Never mind. This is Button." Air burst from his lips along with the broken pieces of a humorless laugh. "I *had* to let Brock go. Multiple people at the kitchen supply store confirmed his alibi, and they caught him on a security camera at a gas station in Mount Vernon on his way up there. He couldn't have been the one to turn Godfrey's gun on him," Easton whispered, surveying the locals as they took notice of him in the back.

"Well, now they're back to Noah." Silas crumpled the empty chip bag and tossed it into the garbage to his left.

"Detective," an older man said as he approached the small group at the back.

Lou didn't recognize him, which meant he probably wasn't a reader. That wasn't necessarily a deal-breaker, but from the way Easton flinched at his greeting, she could already guess she wasn't going to like the man.

"I assume this means you're going to be bringing in Mr. Ramero for questioning now that Mr. Nolan didn't pan out." The older man's weathered eyes narrowed on Easton.

Easton pushed back his shoulders, rising to his full height. "Maurie, you know I won't discuss an ongoing investigation with you."

Maurie's lips fluttered as he exhaled a raspberry. "You're just playing favorites because Noah's your friend."

Noah, who'd walked over after spotting Lou, froze at the sound of his name. His dark eyes tightened with discomfort and flashed to meet Easton's in as much of an apology as he could give him in the crowded space.

But Easton didn't need to handle Maurie. Silas stepped

forward and said, "If you want him to look into anyone who was seen in the neighborhood that day, we could ask why you were wandering around Mrs. Parlor's back garden when her husband was at the dentist."

Maurie's cheeks turned red instantly, and his gaze flicked from Silas to the detective. "I-that's-it's not any of your business," he mumbled, storming off toward the exit.

Silas barked out a triumphant laugh, slapping his hands together to get rid of any remaining chip debris before following Maurie out the door. He gave Lou, Easton, and Noah a salute as he passed by.

Lou pressed her lips together to hide the smile she felt coming on as Noah approached the two of them.

"What was that about?" He frowned.

"I think Silas uncovered an affair, and he used it to save your name from being dragged through the mud any more than it already has." Easton blinked as if he didn't quite believe what had just happened. "Any chance you want me to tell the people the truth about why you were there that night *now*?"

Noah blew out his cheeks. "Even if they knew why I was there that evening, it doesn't change the fact that I walked to Cricket's house at lunch."

Lou curled her fingers into loose fists to keep herself from reaching toward him. She longed to place a hand on his arm or pull him into a comforting hug, but both actions would spread like wildfire in a group this large and this charged with emotion.

"Okay, if you say so." Easton's attention caught to the right, where he spotted Willow helping Cricket with her pile of signs. "I'll see you two later." He slapped a hand on Noah's back as he jogged past him toward his significant other.

Lou jerked her head toward the parking lot and stepped out. Noah followed, but they stayed at least a foot apart, as if knowing getting any closer would be too much of a temptation.

"I had a cat I wanted to discuss with you," Lou said, louder than she needed to, as they spilled out into the crisp fall air. "Would you walk me to my car?"

Noah's lips split into a dimpled grin as anyone within earshot peeled away from them, walking toward their own cars. The lights in the parking lot shone off the rain-slicked pavement, reflecting the many headlights and brake lights as the meeting attendees pulled out.

"So, which cat did you want to discuss?" he asked as they stopped near Lou's car, continuing the ruse even though they didn't need to.

"What are you doing tomorrow?" She knew he usually closed the clinic on Saturdays, but Noah was a busy man. He often worked at his family's quilt shop, and he helped locals with handyman projects. Yet another reason they should trust him, Lou realized.

Noah glanced over his shoulder to make sure there wasn't anyone around, even though Lou had already checked before she'd whispered the question. "Nothing much. Cass has Marigold. I was thinking about tackling the gutters since all those leaves came down this week. Why?"

"Do you think the gutters can wait?" Lou asked. "I was hoping you'd come with me for the day."

Noah's dark brows rose, the sad look from the meeting gone as he tried to figure out what she had planned. "To do what?"

"It's a secret," she whispered. "But I'll tell you when and where to meet me. Just dress comfortably."

A softness took over Noah's eyes as he studied her, and she knew the smile he wore reflected hers. She realized they were doing that thing again, where they were gazing longingly at one another and would likely be found out if they let it go on for too long.

Noah caught it too. "Uh, sure. Yes. That sounds good. I'll see you then." Shooting her a quick wink, he turned on his heel and headed for his car.

Lou couldn't help but chuckle as she climbed into her car and started making plans to cheer up the man she was growing to love.

CHAPTER 7

The next morning, Lou got up early to feed the cats and ensure the shop was ready to go.

"Are you sure you're okay with this?" she asked George as she scanned the place one more time to make sure she hadn't forgotten anything.

George wafted a hand toward the door. "Yes. I'm more than sure. I'm capable of watching the shop for you for one day while you grab your order."

Lou worried her lip. While she'd left the shop here and there for small periods of time, she normally closed if she had to be away for more than a half hour. But she also knew the trip she was going to take was just as important.

Nodding resolutely, Lou said, "You have my number if you have questions."

George adopted her most serious stare. "I do. If one of the cats so much as looks like it might puke, you'll be the first to know. Do you want an hourly update about how many books I sell, or is it okay if I wait until I sell ten before texting?" A teasing smirk took over her lips.

"Ha-ha," Lou said dryly. "You should be nice to me. You'd have just as hard of a time leaving your business behind."

"You're right. I would." George sobered. "Which is exactly why you should trust me." She placed a hand on her heart. "I promise I will treat Whiskers and Words like my very own Technology Emporium."

Hearing that, Lou grabbed her purse, thanked George one last time, and then headed for the back alley where she parked her car. In her purse sat the address of the shipping warehouse in Seattle that was holding two boxes of next week's new releases for her. But the books were just part of the trip.

Lou drove along Pattern Drive and slowed as she reached the playground at the edge of the neighborhood. While it was a popular gathering place for the neighborhood children during the summer and spring months, it was deserted now that it was cold and wet outside.

Well, not completely deserted. Noah sat on one of the swings, making him appear even bigger and burlier than he already did in comparison to the playground equipment. He caught sight of her car and jogged over, slipping into her passenger seat.

"Should I duck until we get out of town?" he asked. But even though his question held the distinct lightness of a joke, Lou could tell he wouldn't be opposed to the idea. "Especially after yesterday. You wouldn't want to get caught with a murder suspect."

The words felt like a stab to Lou's heart. She hated how much this was affecting Noah. Grabbing on to his hand, she squeezed tight. "You are not. Easton knows you're not guilty."

A forceful swallow worked Noah's throat. "And I keep wondering why that doesn't make me feel any better. But just knowing my neighbors think I could've done something like this really has me shaken."

Lou could relate. She'd been treated like a suspect before, but that had been by a detective who hadn't known her. Coming from people Noah interacted with every day, people he thought were his friends, had to sting even more.

"I should've been the one to stay and talk to the police. I'm so sorry. I'm the reason you're in this mess." Lou squeezed his hand once more before beginning the drive toward Seattle.

Scoffing, Noah said, "We did that for me. I'm the one who keeps pushing off telling Cassidy. If we'd been open, none of this would be happening."

Lou hated to see him like this. "Well, let's not worry about it today. Today is all about cheering you up."

"Are you finally going to tell me what we're doing?" His eyes lit up as he looked at her, the happiness in his expression pulling her attention from the road briefly.

"Oh," she said with a giggle. "Well, if George asks, one of my shipments of new releases for next week got held up in the warehouse. It wouldn't ship on time, so I'm making the trip to grab it myself. What *really* happened was that I emailed the fulfillment center, saying I was going to be in town today, and I volunteered to pick it up in person."

Noah's dimpled smile returned, tempting Lou to stare at him instead of the road. Because she couldn't, she grabbed his hand with her free one as she pulled onto the interstate.

"Picking up the boxes at the warehouse will take us about thirty minutes. The rest of the day is ours." She squeezed his hand. "Anything you'd like to do?"

Noah puffed out his cheeks. "I haven't been to the city in longer than I'd like to admit. Honestly, as long as it's with you, I don't care what we do today."

Warmth spread through Lou, relaxing as the distance between them and Button grew. As much as she loved their small town, the anonymity of the city had its own allure, especially when they needed to keep their relationship a secret for a little longer.

Deciding that they would start at the famous Pike Place Market and see where the day took them, Lou parked at a garage nearby, and they walked hand in hand through the crowded stalls. Sneaking through the woods the other night may have felt like they were teenagers, but so did the lovesick way they acted as they wandered through the busy city streets. With any amount of touching being forbidden in Button, they couldn't seem to keep their hands off each other in the city.

Noah's arm was either wrapped around Lou's shoulders, snaking around her waist, or pulling her closer as they stopped to admire something. She leaned up and kissed him whenever she could, the freedom of it feeling delicious. And when Lou found a bookseller in the market, and she tilted her head to the side to read the titles, Noah peppered her exposed neck with soft kisses.

They found a quiet Peruvian lunch spot that felt just as decadent as the rest of the day had been and fed each other bites of the tres leches they shared for dessert. As the day progressed, the stiffness in Noah's shoulders loosened, his laugh became easy once again, and the dimples in his smile deepened.

Lou didn't hear a peep from George, so she sent a quick text after lunch checking in. George's "All good" response gave her enough peace of mind to carry her through the rest of the afternoon.

Noah helped her with the boxes when they decided it was time to stop by the fulfillment center shortly after lunch and offered to drive on the way home. From the way his fingers clutched the steering wheel tighter the closer they got to Button, Lou thought he must be dreading going back.

So it surprised her when he said, "I can't stop thinking about that crime scene."

Lou stared at him for a moment, trying to read his body language to see if she could decide in what context he'd meant the statement. He didn't look scared, or even angry. Determination seemed to tighten his jaw, just as it did with his grip on the wheel.

Ah, so Noah wasn't worried. He was thinking about how to solve the mystery.

"In what way?" Lou asked.

"Just that we must be missing something," Noah answered. "There are a lot of people who hated Godfrey, but the list of those who would kill him has to be short."

"A great way to get the people of Button off your back

would be to help Easton figure out who really killed Godfrey," Lou observed aloud.

Noah kept his gaze forward for the most part, but from the quick glances he stole at her out of the corner of his eye, she could tell she'd hit on exactly what he was thinking.

"You know," Lou said, "I didn't think on it too much because we were all so convinced it was Brock at first, but I think we should look into Diana."

Noah's eyebrows arched up. "Wasn't she out of town?"

"Sure, but things obviously weren't good between the two of them. She went to Vegas by herself, just over a year after they'd gotten married there. Isn't that suspicious?"

Noah contemplated that. "I'd heard that she wanted Godfrey to go with, but he felt like it was too close to the town council meeting and couldn't put the BBS proposal on the line if he couldn't get back in time."

"Maybe even more reason for her to be upset with him. What if this wasn't the first instance of him putting the BBS before her?"

"You know … I was trying to think through anything I could've seen or heard on Wednesday when I stopped by Cricket's house that might be important, and I remembered that when I went into her kitchen to grab her lunch sitting on the counter, I glanced out her kitchen window, which looks through the forest into the Cranes' backyard. I swore I saw a woman with brown hair walking around in the yard, but I thought it was Diana. I didn't know she was out of town."

Lou's heart raced. "That might be something."

Noah peered at her out of the side of one eye. "So, you're on the case?"

She laughed. "*We're* on the case. Yes."

He threaded his fingers through hers, keeping his left hand on the steering wheel. "I mostly care that you're on my side. The killer doesn't stand a chance if you're looking into it."

Lou took the compliment but couldn't help adding, "The two of us made a pretty good team during the last investigation."

"We definitely did." Noah seemed to play through the same memories Lou was reliving. It had been during their last case that they'd finally kissed, after all, breaking the dam of tension that had been building between them for a while.

They stopped for gas in Kirk, switching so Lou was in the driver's seat. She dropped Noah off at the neighborhood park, careful not to let anyone see them as he slipped out of the passenger seat and walked home. It was closing in on five in the evening, so the sun was already setting, giving them the cover of darkness for their drop-off that they'd lacked that morning.

Lou parked behind Whiskers and Words, carrying the first box of books inside. As she kicked open the back door, the sounds of conversation crackled through the shop, as well as the warmth from the fire.

Seeing that Lou had her hands full, George raced over to take the box from her.

"I would've agreed with you before the meeting yesterday, Forrest, but now I think I'm on Cricket's side," George called over her shoulder to the group, then turned to Lou. "Is this it, or are there more boxes?"

"Just one more," Lou said. "I can get it." She narrowed her eyes at the regulars, wondering what they were discussing.

She went to grab the last box from her car and set it next to the first one George had stacked behind the register. It was just about closing time, so it surprised Lou that the entire group of regulars was still there … until she figured out what they were talking about.

"It's not someone from our side. Stop the Vote has to be the killer's attempt to throw Easton off their scent." Cricket crossed her arms. "That's what I would do if it had been me."

Lou shot the woman a warning glare, remembering how scared she'd been when Easton *had* thought it was her, and willing her to stick to her resolution not to run her mouth. At least there were no other customers in the shop to over-hear her.

Forrest swung his head back and forth. "If it's not our side, it's theirs. That goes against everything they want, as does killing Godfrey. He was the one who got their cause further than they had in years. Those people have been trying to keep big businesses out forever. You said it your-self that they had to postpone the vote without Godfrey."

"Ah," Cricket lifted a finger. "But one of my"—she coughed—"sources around town mentioned that the group of them went in on purchasing land together last month. You know that stretch out by the highway that a fast-food chain was looking at developing?"

"So?" Forrest lifted one shoulder. "They bought it together because they all have the goal of keeping those big chains out."

"They didn't *all* buy it together." Cricket cocked an eyebrow. "Godfrey was the only one left out. Or did he refuse? I'd say whatever the reason, it seems like there were more cracks in the BBS than we first realized."

"What do you think, Lou?" Silas lowered his bushy gray eyebrows at her, and the group turned to hear her response. "Which side do you think did this? Forrest and I think it's someone opposed to the BBS, but these two think it's an inside job." He jabbed a thumb toward George and Cricket.

Twisting her lips into a frown, Lou considered what Noah had seen in the backyard. If Diana was in Vegas still that afternoon, another woman had been in the backyard when he'd looked out Cricket's kitchen window. There were two women in the Button Beautification Society. And even though it seemed like a weak string, it was a lead to follow nonetheless.

"I'm not sure," she said. "But I think it's worth looking into the BBS, if only just to rule them out."

"What do you mean, look into them? How do we do that?" George asked.

"We need to infiltrate the BBS." Lou lifted her chin as everyone in the bookshop shot her skeptical glances.

Cricket sniffed. "There's no way they'll let me or anyone who's friends with me on that silly committee. They'd smell subterfuge a mile away."

"It can't be me," George scoffed. "Everyone knows I'm

not changing anything about my business to please some committee members."

Lou must've been on a high from spending such a wonderful day with Noah. And because of that, she felt especially protective of him. If they were going to find the actual killer, they needed to explore all options.

"What about me?" Lou asked, stepping forward. "I didn't sit with you yesterday. I'm still fairly new to town. They don't know how I feel about everything."

Chin descending in a slow nod, Cricket said, "It could work … if you downplay how close we are. Act like we just hang out here without your permission, but we spend enough money that you can't kick us out."

"That's not a bad plan," Silas grumbled, though, from the way his eyebrows slanted down over his eyes, he seemed to hope that wasn't the truth.

"I need to lie so they'll trust me," Lou said, mostly for Silas's benefit. She nodded. "I promise I can do this." Her gaze flicked around the room. "For Easton, of course. If one of them is the killer, he needs this information to solve the case."

Everyone agreed.

"And if Lou gets turned away, we'll keep trying until we get someone inside that group," George said.

Even though Lou agreed, she hoped the first iteration of their plan would work. It had to, for Noah.

CHAPTER 8

The Button Beautification Society must've known they didn't have time to waste. That Sunday, the group met to figure out their next steps. Without Godfrey as their host, they'd resorted to meeting at the Bean and Button.

Lou ordered her regular latte and pretended to be very interested in the community message board hanging in the hallway near their table as she sipped at the to-go cup. She acted wholly uninterested as they complained about the meeting—mostly Cricket and her signs—but when Robin mentioned how they had a week to get more votes, Lou took her chance and pounced.

"I'm so sorry to interrupt, but I heard you mention needing more votes, and I wasn't sure if you were accepting new members."

Sasha Richards practically seethed as she looked Lou up and down. "Why would we let you join? You're friends with the opposition."

Lou snorted. She was tempted to say something flippant about how she couldn't help that they hung out in her shop. Downplaying their friendship had been the plan after all. But as Lou tried to form the words, she found she couldn't make them come out. Voicing such a lie made Lou's stomach turn with discomfort. It was so far from the truth. Those people weren't just her friends, they'd become her family.

She settled on, "My friends allow me to have my own opinions."

Adam Stout ran a hand through his blond hair and sat back. "What could you bring to the group?"

"Having lived in New York City for almost twenty years, I've seen firsthand what it can do to a community when the big corporations come into a neighborhood and kick out the local shops. It kills the soul of the place." She didn't have to lie that time. It really had been her experience. "I've also worked hard to build trust with the community over the past year and a half since I moved here. I think locals respect my opinion and I would add some"—she hesitated as she weighed her words—"I would add a calm presence to a group that's gotten a lot of heat lately for being seen as a little radical."

Mitchell narrowed his eyes. Robin scoffed. And Sasha stood.

"No." Sasha pointed to the door, her long brown hair falling over her shoulder. "Get out. This isn't going to work."

Lou got to her feet in a flash. Normally calm and collected, she felt her frustration rise. Indignation surged through her veins, as she wondered what they were hiding, what they didn't want her to know. It wasn't just about them so blatantly keeping her out. This was about Noah. Her fingers tightened into fists, not because she was going to punch anything, but she needed a place to put her extra energy.

A hand landed on Lou's shoulder. Whirling around, Lou caught Ruby, the manager of the coffee shop, standing behind her. Concern creased the corners of her lips, and she pressed them together in a thin line.

"Hey, I have that order for you. It's in the office." Ruby jerked a thumb behind her. "If you want to follow me..." Ruby's eyes latched on to Lou's, her pupils contracting slightly as she sent her a nonverbal message to go with it.

"Uh, sure." Lou had ordered no such thing but could see something in Ruby's interested gaze that made her sure she needed to play along. "Yeah, that would be great."

With one last glance over her shoulder, Lou followed Ruby down the back hallway and into the Bean and Button office. Although Lou had consumed hundreds of coffees in the shop since she'd moved there, she'd never once set foot in Ruby's office. It was so much like Ruby, Lou almost laughed out loud. The space was organized. Everything had its place. It reminded her so much of the signature braid Ruby's brown hair was always pulled into—contained and controlled.

Ruby motioned for Lou to sit in the chair in the corner across from her desk. She plopped into her office chair.

"Are you sure you don't need to be out front?" Lou

listened to the sounds of the coffee shop spill down the hallway.

"Nah." Ruby's shoulders eased down. "Mary's got it under control. It's you I'm worried about. I've never seen you lose your temper before, and I think I stepped in at just the right time, or you were going to blow."

Ruby's words settled over Lou, and she realized her friend was right. She'd let herself get worked up. She'd always been a fierce partner, supporting her late husband, Ben, in whatever he endeavored to do. But Ben had also been beyond outspoken. He, like Willow, had been loud, confident, and had zero qualms about calling people out when they treated him in ways he didn't appreciate. Noah was different. He had a quiet strength, like her. And she remembered how much it had meant when he'd stood up for her after she'd been accused of murder.

But when Noah had gone to bat for her, he'd done so in a calm, controlled manner. And she needed to do the same. It wouldn't help either of them if she lost it.

Grateful for Ruby's interruption, Lou said, "Thank you for pulling me out of there. This whole situation has really gotten under my skin."

"I know you and Noah are close." Ruby let her dismay show in her down-turned mouth. "It has to be hard to hear people accuse him of this."

For a moment, Lou wondered if Ruby knew about their relationship. She spent a lot of time right across the street from Lou's bookshop after all. Had they slipped up? Made a mistake, and she'd seen them together? But when Lou studied the manager's face, she looked almost as upset as Lou felt.

"It really is," Lou said. "How's Diana holding up with all of this?"

Air rushed through Ruby's lips. "It's hard to tell. She's spending a lot more time around here, which is…" Ruby simply widened her eyes instead of speaking ill of her boss.

Lou understood. Since she'd moved to town, Diana had been much more of a silent owner, letting Ruby run the coffeehouse as she saw fit. Ruby was great at what she did, though, so it never seemed like a bad idea for Diana to give her the reins.

"But that had been going on for a while now, so I don't think it's necessarily in response to Godfrey's death," Ruby added.

"I heard she was in Vegas. Did she say why Godfrey didn't go with?" Even though Noah had already told her what he'd heard, Lou knew there was power in asking questions she *thought* she already had the answers to in an investigation.

Ruby's gaze flicked to the open office door. She leaned over and shoved it closed before answering. "They were supposed to go in the summer, to celebrate their one-year anniversary, but that was right around when Brock bought the mansion, and Diana said Godfrey became obsessed. He said he couldn't leave, that they had to fight this right away." Ruby played with a paperclip on her desk as she spoke. "Apparently, Diana moved the trip twice before she got sick of waiting and went herself."

Lou's eyebrows rose. That information tracked with what Noah had told her. The brown-haired woman Noah had seen that afternoon in the Cranes' backyard was still giving Lou pause as well. It sounded like there was trouble in their marriage, but if Diana was in Vegas during her husband's time of death, the only other option was that she'd hired someone to kill him. Murder was one thing. A contract hit? That seemed far too organized crime for their small town.

Maybe she was grasping because she desperately needed another suspect other than Noah. When she glanced up, Ruby was staring at her.

"I *thought* you might be looking into this one," Ruby said. "But I don't think Diana is responsible for it. We all figured things were hard at home, which was why she'd been coming in more. And now, with Godfrey gone, I think Diana doesn't want to be in that house by herself, so she's been hanging out here. A lot." Ruby's tone grated with fatigue. She quickly added, "Which is great. She's a good boss, and this is her coffee shop. It's just, we've had a year of freedom, and it's hard to go back."

"That makes sense," Lou said, hoping to convey that Ruby shouldn't feel bad for speaking her mind.

"Luckily she had a weekly coffee date with a neighbor today, so I have the morning to myself." Ruby gave Lou a wan smile, which Lou returned.

Despite the frustration earlier after the way the BBS treated her, as well as her lack of movement toward her goal of getting information out of them, Lou realized that she'd learned something important after all. She'd seen Diana as a suspect, but now it sounded like she could drop her and focus her efforts elsewhere.

"Thank you for saving me," Lou said to Ruby. She meant it.

Ruby chuckled. "Anytime."

They opened the office door and headed back into the coffee shop. The BBS had cleared out, so the place wasn't nearly as busy as it had been minutes before. Lou recognized Officers Brenner and Peanut Butter standing at the counter. Officer Brenner was ordering a latte for himself and a puppuccino for Peanut Butter.

It seemed as if Lou and Ruby had ended their break in the office just in time, too, because Diana strode into the Bean and Button at that very moment. Her expression brightened at the sight of Ruby, and she walked forward.

But as she approached the counter, Officer Peanut Butter turned his attention from waiting patiently for his tiny cup of whipped cream, to the owner of the shop. Whereas he'd been standing, tail wagging in anticipation, the bloodhound mix's nose started working, sniffing the air.

The dog sat and let out a loud baying howl, causing everyone in the coffee shop to jump in surprise. Lou expected Officer Brenner to turn red and apologize for the dog's outburst. The young officer did no such thing, however. He studied his canine partner.

It was then that Lou remembered the last time she'd heard Officer Peanut Butter bay like that. It was his signal to his handler that he'd caught a scent.

And the dog was staring straight at Diana Crane.

Lou swallowed, wondering if the dog was barking because Diana lived in the house, so she smelled like the handkerchief. The only other option was that Lou had taken Godfrey's wife off the suspect list too soon.

CHAPTER 9

That afternoon at Whiskers and Words, Lou took advantage of a lull in customers to enter the new releases she'd picked up in the city yesterday into the computer so they'd be ready for their release day that coming Tuesday. She loved the mindless work of entering new books into her system. And with an empty bookshop, she could put on an upbeat mix of music. Even George was gone, helping someone with a laptop that wouldn't turn on.

Lou was just starting on the last title when the bell on the front door rang.

Hope soared inside Lou as she recognized the person who entered. It was Robin Granger from the Button Beautification Society. Had the group changed their mind about Lou's involvement?

The tight frown on Robin's face made Lou rethink her hope, however, wondering instead if the woman had come to scold her for even trying to infiltrate their society.

But that was when Lou noticed the cat carrier at Robin's side.

Every other theory left Lou's mind. This was about a cat, not the BBS. Stepping out from behind the register, Lou pulled her expression into a question as she asked, "What can I do for you? Robin, was it?"

Robin gulped as her gaze flicked down to the plastic carrier she gripped with white knuckles. Instead of answering Lou's question, the woman craned her neck as she glanced around the bookshop, checking for other customers, Lou guessed.

That was confirmed as Robin asked, "Are we alone?"

Lou jerked her head in confirmation, the suspense of the situation skyrocketing at the question.

Robin set the cat carrier on the floor and ran her now-free hands over her face. "I-this is-I'm not…" She closed her eyes and gulped down a steadying breath before she tried again. "I'm wondering if you will take this cat," she finally spat out.

"I mean, of course," Lou said without hesitation. "What's its story? Did you find it outside?"

Even though it had been a lie to explain why he'd been in the woods behind Godfrey Crane's house, Noah hadn't needed to exaggerate the dangers of domesticated animals being outside as the temperature dropped.

At Lou's questions, Robin's mannerisms—already odd —turned downright awkward. She shifted her weight on her feet, and her chest rose and fell as her breathing grew more ragged.

"No," she finally said. "I adopted her."

"I don't understand," Lou said, confused.

"I can't keep her. I thought I would enjoy having a cat, that it would be easy, but it's obviously not for me. She's too wild. Too mean." At that, Robin shoved her arms forward, showing off scratches that marred the insides of both wrists.

Lou bent her knees slightly to get a better look at the gray-and-white cat in the crate. It cowered in the back. She would have to take Robin's word for it, since it wouldn't be something she would find out until the crate was opened, and she wasn't about to do that until she had on some protective gear.

"You can't return her?" Lou asked. "Rescues often have twenty-four-hour policies if the animals don't work out." They had a vested interest in the animals going to suitable homes, and Lou had heard of many of them taking animals back even after years rather than letting them go to unsafe homes.

Robin's jaw clenched tight. "Fine. I didn't rescue her. I bought her. And the place doesn't allow returns."

Lou wondered what kind of place that was, since most breeders she heard of would rather have the animals back than have them stay in bad situations, but she kept her mouth shut. She studied Robin for a moment, wondering what to do next. One thing was clear: she couldn't let the woman who seemed to hate the animal take her back. So, mean or not, Lou would be the best place for the poor creature until she could find it a permanent home.

Lou reiterated her earlier promise. "Sure, I can take her."

If she expected Robin to relax at her agreement to take the cat, she was disappointed. Instead of softening in relief, Robin tensed further.

"The thing is," Robin said. "I was wondering if you wouldn't mind keeping this a secret from the rest of the town. I don't want them to think I'm someone who abandons cats."

Except that you are. Lou kept the words inside.

"Don't do it, Lou," George's voice called out from the back of the shop, making Lou jump.

Robin stiffened.

"Sorry to listen in," George said as she walked forward. "But I came in through the back while this one was asking you to lie for her. And you can't do it."

Robin's nostrils flared. She was about to reach for the cat crate when George's hand shot out to stop her.

"At least, not without something in return," George added. Her lips pulled into a side smile, and she cocked an eyebrow at Robin.

"What do you want?" Robin's tone was tight, but if she was upset, it wasn't enough to leave without hearing out George.

"Let Lou join your silly society." George folded her arms in front of her.

Robin's mouth parted. "Why would you want that? You're actively opposed to our goals."

George scoffed, "Sure, but Lou isn't. Being friends doesn't mean we have to agree on everything. And this seems important to her. She was really sad earlier when you told her she couldn't join."

Robin scanned the shop, as if one of the books might hold the answer to help her get out of the situation she was in. Finally, she said, "Okay, I'll talk to them." Her gaze cut from George, to Lou, to the cat crate. "But if you say anything to anyone about this, I'll kick you out myself."

Lou bobbed her head.

"Our next meeting is tomorrow at the Bean and Button. Nine. We had to call yesterday's early because we couldn't hear over all the noise in the coffeehouse." With that, Robin turned on her heel and left, cat crate and all just sitting on the floor at Lou and George's feet.

Unsure whether to whoop in triumph or cry at the sadness of the situation, Lou knelt next to the cat crate. Robin and her angry energy must've held the other cats at bay, because now that she was gone, they wandered over with eyes wide and noses sniffing at the air.

"That was pretty quick thinking," Lou told George.

George bowed forward in a nonverbal *you're welcome.* "Should we let her out?"

"I don't think so. You missed the first part of the conversation, but the reason Robin is getting rid of her is that she's mean. Robin had scratches all down her arms." Lou pulled her phone out of her back pocket. "I'll see if Noah can come check her out."

Angling her phone away from George so she wouldn't be able to read any of the texts between Lou and Noah that were ... less cat related, Lou sent him a quick update.

Hey, new cat just came in. If you have time later or even tomorrow, I'd love for you to check her out. Maybe bring a mild sedative too? The owner who dropped her off said she's mean.

As she sent the message, a fresh wave of indignation rose inside Lou. Noah responded, seeming to share in her feelings.

Owner? Dropped off? I can tell I'm already not going to like this story. My last appointment is at four. I'll come after that.

Lou texted back a thank-you. "Noah's going to come by and check her out after he's done with his appointments for the day."

George assessed the cat carrier. "Do you really think she's mean?"

Chewing on her lip, Lou couldn't say. "I'm not sure why Robin would buy her if she was so mean. But she said she was sweet in the store." She shrugged. "At least with us she'll be in excellent hands."

"I can watch things down here if you want to take her upstairs and let her wander, see how she reacts." George dropped her purse behind the checkout counter.

Lou took a beat to consider before accepting George's offer. With the cat crate at her side, Lou headed for the back staircase.

"You can let Geralt down. That way, the two of you can be alone," George called after Lou.

Lou had almost forgotten that Geralt was confined

upstairs. As much as she loved the guy, unless she wanted to wear him around like George did, she couldn't have him down in the bookshop when his owner was gone.

The gray-and-white cat waited by the door at the bottom of the staircase as Lou unlocked and opened it, as if he'd heard George's voice. He hesitated for a moment to sniff the crate Lou held before trotting over to his owner, meowing a greeting almost the whole way.

"Why, hello, my precious boy," George cooed to him. "I missed you too."

Lou chuffed out a laugh at the interaction before she ascended into the apartment. Making sure the door was closed behind her, Lou set the crate on the floor in the living room, opened the little metal door, and then stepped back. She knew it wasn't out of the question for a cat to be so aggressive that it would attack a human. But the fact that this one had been nice enough in the shop where Robin had purchased her told Lou that, even if she was "mean," she probably wasn't going to come after Lou unprovoked.

Making a mug of tea, Lou brought it over to the couch and settled next to the window overlooking the gray, slightly rainy streets outside. She pulled a blanket off the back of the couch and tucked it under her feet. Cozy as could be, Lou picked up the book she was reading off her coffee table. It was a fantasy, and the author did such an amazing job of pulling her into the world, that Lou felt like she'd been transported out of her apartment and into the story.

She hadn't meant to get so distracted, but a half hour went by before Lou's phone buzzed next to her, startling her out of the world of magic and adventure. Checking the clock, she knew it wouldn't be Noah yet. He was likely just starting his last appointment. The message was from George.

How's it going up there?

Lou glanced at the crate in the middle of the space and inhaled. It was empty. She'd been so focused on her book that she'd missed the cat's exit from the open carrier. Trying not to panic, Lou stayed put on the couch, but her eyes scanned the room, searching for the small feline.

She found her over by the water and food dishes Lou always had out for the cats near the kitchen.

The cat was drinking, her back hunched as she glanced around the room. From her posture, it looked like she expected someone or something to come grab her at any moment. Lou's heart went out to her.

Just a few months ago, she'd acquired her newest cat. While Meatball was comfortable with Lou, the cat had been on the street and must've had some terrible experiences with men, because she cowered anytime a man was around. Well, not *every* man. Meatball loved Noah, and was getting much more comfortable with Forrest and Silas. Because of her past, Lou and her regulars celebrated every small victory.

In the same vein, Lou felt like this cat even being out of its crate was a great first step.

She carefully took a picture and sent it to George, who responded right away.

Aww. She's so small. She looks like a tiny
Geralt.

They had similar coloring with the blotches of white mixed into a blueish-gray coat. Lou sent a message in return.

She has the longest whiskers I've ever
seen! They're so fluffy.

George sent back an emoji with huge, watery eyes, showing that she thought it was just as cute as Lou did.

That taken care of, Lou exchanged her phone for her book once more and lost herself in the story just as quickly as she had before. But this time she caught movement out of the corner of her eye when the cat slunk across the living room. Lou stilled as the diminutive thing locked its golden eyes on her. It froze where it was, one paw in the air. Slowly, the cat arched its back and let out a wet hiss.

Lou turned her attention back to her book, realizing it had been the eye contact that had made the cat uncomfortable. She monitored the animal in her peripheral vision as it moved once more, slinking over to the window. It hesitated before jumping onto the low sill.

And even though it perched there, much like the other cats did in the evenings, its tail twitched, showing Lou it wasn't relaxing just yet.

CHAPTER 10

Footsteps clomped up the stairs a short while later, too heavy to belong to George. Lou set down her book, careful not to make any sudden movements. The cat was still in the window, but it arched its back once again as Noah appeared in the doorway.

His gaze locked on Lou first. The sun itself seemed to shine in his dimpled smile, making her heart melt. She stood, walking over to meet him. And even though George hadn't followed him up the stairs—there were still fifteen minutes before the bookshop would close for the day—she didn't dare kiss him with the window shades up as they were. It was a gloomy day outside, and Lou didn't fool herself into thinking people couldn't see right in if they tried hard enough.

"Windows," she said as his eyes narrowed when she stopped a few feet away from him.

He nodded in understanding, his attention finally

settling on the cat, possibly because it was in the window, but also because it began hissing at him just as it had with Lou earlier.

"She's not a fan of eye contact." Lou gave him a wink.

He chuckled. "I can see that."

Opening the bag he'd brought with him, he pulled out a small packet. It reminded her of the goop runners sometimes consumed to give them energy in the middle of a race. He grabbed the food bowl from the floor in the kitchen and placed it on the counter, squeezing a meaty-smelling puree out of the goo packet and then mixing in the crushed bits of a sedative tablet from a medicine bottle that he must've prepped back at the clinic.

Noah set the concoction down and motioned toward the couch with a jerk of his head. "Let's encourage her to move toward the food and see if she'll eat. That'll take a while to get into her system, so you can tell me the story while we wait."

Lou followed Noah as he walked toward the couch. And even though he didn't make any movement to reach for the cat or even stare at her, his proximity did the trick. She hissed once more as he settled onto the couch, and then she jumped down from the window. Lou reclaiming her seat at the other end of the couch made the cat slink across the apartment so she could have her space.

For a moment, Lou worried she would slip down onto the stairs, and they would have to figure out a way to convince her to come back up, but she smelled the rich puree Noah had placed in the food bowl. Her pink nose worked as she caught the scent, and then she appraised the humans as she crossed over to the bowl. Moving so she could monitor them while she ate, she perched next to the bowl just as she'd done with the water, and ate.

The self-satisfied smile Noah adopted as he turned back to face Lou made her wish she could pull him into a kiss. Instead, she reached a foot across the couch to nudge him.

"You're pretty good at this. You should consider a career in working with animals," she teased.

Noah's grin turned wicked. He grabbed at her foot, catching it between his large hands. His arms tensed, like he was considering using the foot to pull her over to him. But his gaze flicked over to the windows and he refrained. He kept her foot, however, strong fingers kneading into it as he massaged it through the wool sock. People on the streets wouldn't be able to see that.

"I don't think she's mean." Lou sank back into the couch, reveling in the foot massage.

Noah hummed in agreement. "Whenever I hear people talk about animals like that, it's always fear. So, who dropped her off?" His dark eyebrows lowered as he prepped himself for a story he already knew he wouldn't enjoy.

"Robin Granger," Lou said.

"From Button Storage?" Noah's dark eyes shot open with surprise.

"And the BBS," Lou added. "But we can't let anyone else know this was her cat. She doesn't want to be known as a person who abandons an animal because it's hard to deal "with." Lou congratulated herself for not rolling her eyes as she repeated the woman's plea from earlier.

"Even though that's what she is," Noah snorted. "She doesn't get to ask that of you."

Lou inclined her head. "I was about to tell her the same thing, but George walked in just at that moment and told her we would keep her secret if she convinced the rest of the BBS to let me join."

Considering that for a moment, Noah said, "Which means this morning didn't go well?"

Lou pressed her lips into a tight line, remembering how frustrated she'd gotten with them. "No."

The muscles of his throat tensed as he swallowed. "Okay, we can keep it a secret, then. She didn't tell anyone else that she'd gotten a cat?"

"I guess not. Which means she couldn't have had her for that long."

Noah exhaled a frustrated breath through his nose. "She bought her and then decided she didn't like her?"

"Apparently she was nicer at the pet shop."

Checking over his shoulder, Noah watched as the cat licked up the last of the food. Her posture had already relaxed, and she sank onto her feet instead of hunching like she would run at any moment.

He turned back to Lou, fingers kneading into the arch of her foot. "They could've had her mildly sedated in hopes she'd sell."

"Which would make sense why they had a no-return policy."

"Right. Did Robin give you the details for the next

meeting?"

"She did. Now we just have to figure out what I'm looking for."

As if on cue, the doorway at the bottom of the stairs opened and closed, signaling George's ascent. Noah gave Lou's foot one last squeeze before she pulled it back to her side of the couch.

George's footsteps slowed at the top of the stairwell. Her head poked around the wall, and she scanned the apartment as if she were searching for monsters.

For a moment, Lou wondered if George's hesitation to walk into the apartment was because she wasn't sure if they would be kissing. The thought sent hot and cold shivers through Lou. But then George's gaze locked on to the cat over by the kitchen and she relaxed. Scooting around the dining table, George gave the cat as wide of a berth as she could before plopping into one of the armchairs across from the couch in the living room.

The cat, done eating and in the middle of cleaning her face, froze and watched George. Once the young woman had taken a seat, the cat went back to licking her paw and running it along her whiskers.

"So ... what's the verdict? Is she healthy?" George asked Noah.

"I haven't done the exam yet. I snuck a sedative into the food she just ate, so I have to wait for that to take effect before I attempt to do anything with her." He examined his hands. "I'd rather not get bitten and scratched to pieces."

"How are the rest of the cats?" Lou asked, knowing

most of them followed her up into the apartment in the evenings.

George let out a rough chuckle. "Oh, they're mad. None more than Geralt. But they'll be fine."

The cats had tons of soft places to lay, food, water, and litter boxes down there. It was more about the company, she guessed. Save for Catnip Everdeen, they were all very social cats who liked to be around people, and they followed accordingly. Even Catnip, who sometimes stayed down in the bookshop at night, usually ventured upstairs to curl up on the couch.

"We were just discussing what Lou's going to need to look for at the BBS meeting you were clever enough to get her an invitation to." Noah cocked an eyebrow at George in a silent *well done.*

Rubbing her hands together, George said, "Ah, yes. Well, I think poking them about the land they bought together would be a good first step. Maybe there's a good reason Godfrey wasn't included in that purchase."

Noah, who hadn't yet heard about that information, listened as George filled him in.

"I wonder if they'll even tell me about that." Lou chewed on her lip. "It sounded like Cricket had to dig quite a bit to get that news. It's not something just anyone knows."

Noah's eyes lit up. "It would be if you were considering purchasing land too. Hypothetically, of course. Maybe you had your eye on that piece, but it was taken off the market and you asked who bought it. Cass could easily find that out."

For a moment, Lou wondered if Cass hadn't been Cricket's "source" in the first place. "The bookshop is doing well, but not *that* well." Lou wrinkled her nose. "I think it might seem suspicious if I start talking about buying up large plots of commercial real estate around Button when everyone knows I put a lot of my savings into this place."

"True. What about someone who has money to spare?" Noah asked, an excited glimmer in his eye.

Lou didn't have to think too hard about who Noah was referring to. There weren't many people who could purchase land—or a newspaper—on a whim. Sebastian Andrade, a local millionaire, had recently broken away from his family's historically reclusive ways. He'd liked the feeling of being part of the community so much that he'd jumped in to save the *Button Post* a few months ago when the editor and chief had abruptly quit.

"Everyone knows Sebastian listens to you, Lou," George said. "If you said you were asking around about properties for him, I doubt anyone would think twice."

Chewing her lip, Lou contemplated the idea. "That could work, though I'd want to give Sebastian a heads-up before I used him in the story. He's got enough on his plate right now trying to find a new editor in chief and I don't want to complicate his life."

Noah bowed his head forward in agreement.

Lou pulled out her phone.

> Hey, any way you would mind if I told people I was looking out for a good commercial property for you to buy in town?

Sebastian may have been a busy millionaire, but he was always a prompt texter. Right away, she received a response.

> Only if you tell me the story behind the request soon. Over dinner?

Lou hesitated. She'd already told him she had feelings for Noah months ago when Sebastian had asked her out. Though he didn't know that they'd officially gotten together, she didn't want to have to remind him that she—

But she didn't need to, because another text followed that one.

> You, Noah, Willow, Easton, and George. How about it? A friends' dinner tomorrow night?

Lou breathed out relief. If Noah caught the worry that had flitted across her face, he didn't mention it.

"He says yes, but in return, he wants us to come over for dinner tomorrow," Lou explained.

George scoffed, "Twist my arm."

"Yeah," Noah said, "I hate gourmet food and a beautiful view of the valley." He winked at Lou.

She texted back that she'd have to check with Willow and Easton, but that George and Noah were in.

"Okay, so I'm ready to do some digging at the meeting tomorrow."

Noah cocked an eyebrow as he checked over his shoulder at a very sleepy cat tucked into a loaf right next to the empty food bowl. "And it looks like this little lady's ready for her exam."

As Noah carefully stood from the couch, George asked Lou, "What are you going to name her?"

A smirk split Lou's face as she studied the cat. "I was thinking Hermeowone Granger."

George laughed. "That's perfect. That'll show Robin."

While, to the rest of the town, it would just seem as if Lou had chosen another literary character, like Catnip Everdeen, sharing the last name Granger with Robin would be a constant reminder to the woman of the cat she'd abandoned.

"You know," Noah said, clearing his throat. "There are people who might've just abandoned the cat outside if they didn't want it anymore. I think Robin deserves credit for bringing it to a place where she knew the cat would be safe and well cared for."

Lou swallowed, guilt rising around her throat in hot waves. "You're right, Noah." She shook her head. "I didn't even think about that."

"I feel like a jerk." George wrinkled her nose.

Noah chuckled. "Don't. I just wanted to remind you that I often see evidence of people who make far less compassionate decisions in the face of the same circumstances. There are also a lot more instances than you'd think that result in people having to give up their beloved pets, so I always try to keep an open mind."

Just one more reason Lou had fallen for the man. The reminder made her want to wrap her arms around him, but she controlled the impulse with George there.

"Should I choose a different name?" Lou asked.

Noah shrugged. "I still like Hermeowone."

Lou smiled. "Me too. How about we think of it as a way to honor her previous owner for making the right decision when she brought her here?"

George and Noah agreed, and the name was officially settled.

CHAPTER 11

Lou was so anxious about the meeting the next day, she couldn't stop glancing across the street at the Bean and Button.

"Why don't you just go early? I can watch the place for a little longer," George said, hand on her hip. "Especially if it means I don't have to endure your fidgeting for an extra half hour," she added under her breath.

Shooting an eye roll toward the young woman, Lou shook her head. "I can't be the first one. In fact, I think I need to wait until I see Robin show up. What if she hasn't warned them about me yet?" Waiting would guarantee the least amount of confusion all around.

George pursed her lips. "You're probably right."

So Lou paced, staying put as Adam and Mitchell entered the coffee shop, followed shortly by Sasha.

Watch, Robin won't even show, Lou thought incredulously as the clock ticked toward nine.

As if she'd called on the universe for just the right thing, Robin walked down the street at that very moment.

"That's my cue." Lou waved to George, her nerves making the motion more frantic than she meant to.

"Good luck," George called.

Lou waited for a car to pass before jogging across the street and slipping into the bustling coffee shop. In addition to the crowds of people hoping for a Monday morning pick-me-up, the hundreds of plastic buttons covering the walls overwhelmed Lou after the cozy, quiet atmosphere of the bookshop. There, an errant meow or spirited conversation between customers were the loudest sounds she would hear all day. Here, the scream of the milk steamer, the chewing growl of the coffee grinder, and the conversation between Ruby and her barista caused the customers seated at the various tables to raise their voices to be heard.

Despite the visual and auditory busyness, the roasted smell of coffee pulled Lou forward. As did the promise of answers. Once Lou had ordered, she wandered over to the table the BBS had claimed near the front window.

Robin went rigid as Lou approached, her gaze flicking between her and the other members as her cheeks turned pink.

Ah, so I was right. She didn't warn them. Lou was glad she'd stuck with her plan to show up after Robin, then.

But if Lou was hoping for the woman to jump up to introduce her, she was sorely disappointed. In fact, Robin sipped her coffee and acted like it was the most interesting thing she'd ever seen.

Sasha sneered up at Lou. "You again?"

"Didn't you get the hint yesterday?" Adam asked.

Wetting her lips, Lou glared at Robin.

Robin must've realized she wasn't getting out of this, because she finally glanced up from her coffee. "I, uh, well, Lou may have convinced me that we should give her a chance."

Lou raised her hands. "It can be a trial if you'd like. What about one meeting? Then you can decide if you think I'm a good fit."

The society members frowned, checking with one another.

Finally, Mitchell said, "Fine. One meeting. And then we get to decide if you stay: all of us ... not just Robin," he added.

Lou took a seat, hoping that was enough of an agreement for them.

Just then, the barista banged the porta filter on the counter to get rid of the excess grounds. Sasha jumped. Mitchell closed his eyes in frustration. Robin massaged her temple. Lou remembered how Robin had said they'd had to cut their meeting short the day before because of the noise, and that had been before Officer Peanut Butter had even started his barking.

An idea came to Lou. "You know," she said, dragging out the word. "We could always meet at my bookstore. It's much quieter, and I have a table I can set up for us in the back." George's Dungeons and Dragons club met there most Sundays.

She could tell it was an effort for them to keep the scowls off their faces at her offer. A few of them glanced across the street, sending longing looks at the adorable bookstore. In the gloomy fall morning, the orange glow of the stove in the corner and the warm light from the interior lamps spilled out of the windows. Two cats were lounging in the windows, and Sapphire's white fur was visible from where he was curled on the small table in the front of the shop.

Two gorgeous white oak trees in large pots flanked the windows, on loan from Valley Nursery. While Willow had been loaning Lou trees for the entrance to the bookshop since before she'd opened the nursery, the quality of the plants had increased immensely. When Willow had still been a high school horticulture teacher, the trees she brought Lou were often in need of help—either blooming too early, too late, or not blooming at all. Coming to the bookstore was a last resort to see if a difference in scenery would help.

Now that Willow owned the nursery, some of her best stock came to Lou. Not only was there a plaque in front of each pot explaining where they were on loan from, but they were also for sale. Lou could collect the money for the plants right there in the bookshop if there was an interested buyer. Likewise, Lou had pulled some of Willow's favorite gardening books and had put them in the nursery for people to purchase without having to make an extra trip down the street.

The oak tree's leaves were crimson and gold, making them appear frozen in flames. The colors danced in the eyes of the BBS members.

"Maybe we could *try* it." Adam wrinkled his nose, as if he expected to get backlash from suggesting such a thing.

It was as if Ruby could hear what was happening at the table, and knew Lou needed help, because she chose that moment to drop the stainless-steel frothing container. It clattered along the counter, making half the people jump in surprise.

"Apologies, everyone," Ruby called with an contrite grin.

At that, Sasha said, "Let's try it."

The BBS stood.

"Can we bring our drinks?" Mitchell asked.

Lou smiled. "Sure thing."

She walked in front of the group as they headed out the front door and crossed the street. George must've been monitoring the coffee shop, because as Lou reached the other side of the street, George met her gaze through the front window, eyes widening with excitement.

Lou thought about asking if anyone was allergic to cats but thought better of it. Not only was the bookstore, and the felines who were housed within, well known around town, Lou also had a warning sign on the door. If the BBS had agreed to move the meeting to the shop, they knew what they were stepping into.

"Hey, the coffeehouse was a little loud, so we're going to reconvene over here," Lou explained to George with a sly wink.

"Let me help you with the table." George strode ahead of Lou. She was used to the special quirks of the folding table and could open it without pinching her fingers, a feat Lou couldn't always claim.

Glancing back at the group, Lou didn't miss the way Robin scanned the bookshop, her worried eyes settling on each cat. It was as if she worried that Hermeowone would remember her and sneak up on her, finally exacting her revenge.

At least the cat's exam with Noah had gone well the previous evening. She'd still hissed, and Lou had to wrap her into a towel like the contents of the angriest little burrito, but Noah was able to conclude that she was healthy, flea free, microchipped, and if the scar on her belly was any indication, she'd also been spayed. She was, however, incredibly scared.

"She doesn't seem feral, so her fear definitely seems to have been born from experience with humans," Noah had said when Lou asked if he thought it could've been Robin who hurt her. "I don't think it's something she developed over the last few days. But possibly Robin didn't help."

For the sake of the meeting, Lou told herself it couldn't have been Robin who hurt Hermeowone. Mostly because she wouldn't be able to sit in the same room as the woman if she had.

While George set up the table, Lou unfolded the chairs they kept in the back hallway, ushering the BBS members into them as she placed them around the table. A customer walked in, and George scurried up front to help them while Lou focused on the group in front of her.

"So, where were we?" She smiled.

Adam's eyelids fluttered, mirroring his stutter when he

said, "Uh ... I, uh ... Mitchell was going to fill us in on what he learned about possible workarounds if we can't get the votes needed at the upcoming meeting."

Lou rested her elbow on the table, setting her chin on top of her hand as she acted as intrigued as she could about the matter at hand.

Mitchell inclined his head a touch. "I was able to talk to Kyle, and he said the town bylaws require all measures to go through a six-month waiting period before trying again. Which means, we're probably looking at a year before we could even hope to get on a ballot again."

Based on the dejected whispers that flitted through the group, they'd been holding out hope that there would be a quicker option.

"That means we have to get out there and gather as many votes as we can for this round." Sasha cut a warning glare at Lou. "Using whatever means necessary."

Warning bells rang in Lou's mind. Was that what they'd done with Godfrey? Had he pulled out of their land deal, leaving them unsure if they could count on him?

Adam rubbed his hands together. "My family can be *very* convincing." The gleam of something insidious in his eye made her shiver.

Stuffing her worry, Lou said, "My best friend, Willow, just opened Valley Nursery this past spring. I'll see if I can get her on our side. Also..." Lou paused. "I'm not sure what the bylaws say, but I'm wondering if it might be possible to have the vote anonymous."

"Why?" Robin asked.

"Well, I'm good friends with Noah Ramero, and I think

he might also be sympathetic to our cause, but Cricket Marshall is like an aunt to him." Lou left it at that, not wanting to spell it out completely.

George coughed from the front of the store, shooting Lou a sidelong glance. Lou had a feeling she would get a congratulatory pat on the back from the young woman after the meeting was over.

From the looks of the BBS members, Lou would deserve it. What had started out as wary glares softened. Not only had Lou offered her space, but she seemed to be even more helpful than they originally expected.

"That's not a bad idea," Mitchell said. "The pressure to vote a certain way could hurt us."

Sasha frowned. "But that changes the dynamic completely."

"True. But I have a good feeling that it's going to be for the better." Lou made a show of lowering her voice. "The opposition is loud and has a lot of social pull in the town."

Lou caught the sly smile that tugged at George's lips from across the room before the young woman busied herself with a stack of books that needed to be shelved. Lou was careful not to promise anything she wasn't willing to back up. And even though her cryptic comments seemed to do the trick of convincing the BBS, by the end of the meeting, she hadn't committed to anything real.

They eventually all agreed with her, Mitchell promising to talk to Kyle about the possibility. The rest of them fidgeted, like they were about to leave since the meeting was over.

"Oh." Lou placed her fingertips against her temple. "I meant to ask something before we leave."

The group, once unsure of her membership, waited to hear what she had to say. Lou hoped her question wasn't about to completely undo the goodwill she'd worked so hard to build between them.

"Sebastian Andrade, someone who is also interested in our cause, is hoping to pick up some commercial land in town." Lou held a hand up to her mouth. "Don't spread it around, because it's not a done deal yet, but he's hoping to open an animal shelter. You know what a heart he has for stray cats and all."

The group members—especially Robin and Sasha—swooned a little at the mention of the handsome billionaire.

"Anyway," Lou continued. "He wanted me to ask the lot of you because he mentioned that you all had purchased a sizeable chunk of it together out on the northern end of Pattern Drive earlier this year. He wasn't sure if you had plans for that or if it was just a bid to keep it out of a corporation's hands."

The group glanced at each other, some of their earlier guardedness returning. But her work wasn't completely undone, and with a few slight nods, they seemed to agree that it was okay to acknowledge.

Well, everyone but Robin. The woman clammed up, turning a bright shade of red.

With Robin suddenly silent, Adam was the one who spoke up. "We would love to talk to him about selling. He guessed right. We heard a big-box store was sniffing around the property and, with this proposition not yet passed, we couldn't keep them out unless we came in and bought it before they did."

Nodding, Lou said, "Great, I'll let him know he can get in touch with you." She swept an index finger across the table. "All of you went in on the property together?"

They confirmed with various dips of chins and grunts of acknowledgment.

"Does Godfrey's death complicate that? Will the property be stuck until lawyers deal his portion? Or does it revert to Diana?" Lou asked.

Gazes sliding to one another, Adam again seemed to be the spokesperson for the group, because he said, "Godfrey didn't purchase the property with us."

Lou's mouth formed a surprised O.

"He … wasn't sympathetic to our cause, in that way." Sasha scrunched up her nose.

"He wasn't?" Lou asked. "Isn't that, like, your entire cause?"

Mitchell pulled a sharp breath through his nose and tilted his head in a motion that said *she's not wrong*.

But Robin held up a hand to stop him, apparently finally having found her voice. "Godfrey's goals aligned with ours in certain ways. He was the conduit we needed. We couldn't care less about the sewing theme but recognize that having those stipulations will make it harder for corporations to intrude." Her words spilled out in a rush, as if she knew she was saying too much, but her nerves were getting the best of her. "It became a means to an end," she said to finish, pressing her lips together like that might stop her from blurting anything else.

Lou tucked away the information. Even more interesting was the discomfort she noticed in Robin. Despite sounding sure of their mission, Robin's shoulders hunched in much the same way that they had when she'd dropped off Hermeowone the day before. Sasha became very interested in her nails. And Adam had a throat-clearing tick when he got nervous.

Cricket had been right. There was something there. And she was going to get to the bottom of it.

The person who intrigued her the most, however, was Robin Granger. The woman practically ran out once the meeting was finished. A reaction Lou guessed had nothing to do with her abandoned cat sitting upstairs.

CHAPTER 12

If Lou thought the view from Sebastian Andrade's mansion on the hill had been beautiful in the summer, it was positively breathtaking in the fall. The reds, yellows, and oranges she'd been admiring in the oak trees outside her bookshop were splattered across the Skagit Valley as it stretched out before them. Puffs of smoke from fires twisted through the cool November air. The sun was just beginning to set as Sebastian led the group of friends into the living room.

"I love fall," Willow said as she walked up to the enormous picture windows along the eastern wall of the house. Her chest puffed out with a searching inhale as if she were trying to smell the woodsmoke from inside. Easton walked over to her, wrapping an arm around her shoulder.

The scents inside the house were doubly enticing. Smells of garlic and herbs pulled the crew farther into the living room. Besides the view, the inside of the house held even more treasures, at least in Lou's humble opinion. Cats lounged on almost every surface in the house, it seemed. But Lou zeroed in on one.

"Hi, Catticus." She knelt to greet the lean gray tabby.

The mischievous feline had started out with her at the bookshop, but he'd been too active for the quiet store. Between leaping from the tops of shelves and racing between customers' legs, it had been clear Catticus needed a home where his athletic talents weren't only encouraged but supported. Sebastian's home, full of custom cat trees, climbing equipment, and platforms running across every wall, was perfect.

It was actually how Meatball had come to live with Lou. Sebastian had found her in the city, but hadn't realized the extent of her fear of men until he had her home and saw how much more comfortable she was with women.

"He's doing well," Sebastian answered for the cat. "A true athlete, that one. And how's Meatball?"

Lou grinned. "Wonderful. I've got Silas and Forrest working on winning her over." She shot a sidelong glance at Noah, knowing he'd been helping, too, during the evenings he visited before George had moved in.

"Meat seems like a social butterfly compared to your newest cat," George said as she walked past Lou and Noah, toward a black cat splayed out on the sectional couch.

Sebastian's eyebrows hitched higher. "I want to hear all about it, but dinner's ready, so we should sit." He waved for the group to follow him into the dining room, where the delicious aromas only intensified.

But George, normally won over by the promise of food,

froze as she entered the dining room in front of Lou. "What are you doing here?"

Stepping around George, Lou recognized Wesley Saint James, Sebastian's private investigator. He sat at the table, sipping on a glass of wine, fixing George with a roguish smirk.

"Pining for you, George, darling," he said in a flirty tone Lou was sure would drive her young friend mad.

George huffed in response, taking the seat farthest away from Wesley.

Lou and Willow exchanged a glance that was half worried anticipation and half excitement of how the dinner might go, now that those two were in the same room. The two had butted heads ever since the moment they'd met … on a date. They'd called off the date almost instantly, deciding there was nothing between them, but by the fire that sprang up anytime they were around one another, Lou guessed there might be more chemistry than they first thought—only the explosive kind that might clear a building.

"Nice to see you, Wesley," Lou said as she took the seat across from him. "What *are* you actually doing here, though?" She repeated George's question from earlier. She didn't mean to be rude, but the question poked the back of her mind.

Sebastian took the seat next to Wesley, slapping a hand on the young man's shoulder. "Wes has been helping a lot with the newspaper, actually, vetting the editor candidates I've been looking through. But with this Crane shooting, I figured I'd let him loose on a real mystery for a bit."

Easton cleared his throat as he slid into the chair next to Willow.

"All to help the police, of course, Detective." Sebastian bowed his head humbly toward Easton.

Skepticism flitted across Easton's features. Because of the seat George chose, Noah was left to sit next to Wesley. He kept his focus on the napkin and place setting in front of him as he attempted to hide the grin twitching the corners of his mouth.

Surprising everyone at the table, instead of telling Sebastian and Wesley to back off, Easton asked, "So? Has he found anything?"

Every gaze cut to Easton in surprise.

"What?" He shrugged. "Can't hurt to ask. We're at a bit of a standstill. We've questioned the entire Forest Pond neighborhood, the Button Beautification Society, the construction crew that was at the mansion that day, and Diana Crane. Either no one saw anything, or someone's lying to me. It's part of the reason I'm particularly interested to see if anything comes from Lou's efforts."

Sebastian's eyes glinted. He leaned forward, resting his chin on the heel of his hand. "Oh? And what are Lou's efforts? I'm guessing this has to do with the favor you asked of me."

Lou glanced over at Easton, having told him her plan to infiltrate the BBS during the drive to Sebastian's. "I've joined the Button Beautification Society. Cricket is convinced that someone in the group killed Godfrey, so I figured it couldn't hurt to pretend to be sympathetic to their cause and poke around a little to see if any of them have a motive."

"They were the last ones to see Godfrey alive, and they left him out of that land deal," Easton said.

Wesley pressed his lips forward, impressed. "And have you found anything yet?"

George grunted. "Only that the whole BBS went in on a piece of commercially zoned property out on Pattern Drive on the edge of town, except Godfrey."

"And they mentioned he didn't have the same vision as they did. That they only overlapped in certain areas." Lou focused on Sebastian and Wesley as she spoke, having filled in the rest of the group during the car ride up there.

"Ah, so that's why I needed to be interested in commercial properties." Sebastian seemed to pout for a moment. "But you didn't even have to dig to find that out? They just handed that information over?"

Easton nodded, having called it out as suspicious as well. Motioning to the platters of food set out on the table, Sebastian started serving himself, so the others did as well. The spread was a veritable feast, with two different baked-pasta dishes, along with broccoli and a creamy mushroom chicken.

"Yes, but most concerning was Robin Granger." Lou served herself a piece of chicken as she spoke. "After I asked about the land deal, she ran out of there like she was being chased by a swarm of bees." Lou left it at that. Even though George and Noah knew she'd been the one to drop off Hermeowone, that didn't mean Lou had to keep breaking her promise to keep her identity a secret.

Sebastian shot a glance over at Wesley, who'd just shoved a forkful of pasta in his mouth.

"You never answered my question about what Wesley knows," Easton reminded Sebastian, his tone firm, showing he still controlled the situation. He could tell them all to shut down any side sleuthing at any moment, and they would have to listen.

"Well, I know Robin's not the killer," Wesley said after he swallowed the rather large bite he'd taken.

George snorted. "How do you know that?"

"I was following her during the time Godfrey was killed." Wesley sent her a lazy smile, winking in her direction.

"Why were you following her?" Easton's voice held a hint of warning, but his eyes were full of intrigue.

Sebastian's chin settled low. "I asked him to. He's following all my editor candidates."

"Editor candidates?" Willow asked, shock making the question come out louder than she meant to.

Their host confirmed, saying, "Both Robin and Mitchell have applied."

"Mitchell has an alibi," Easton supplied. "He volunteers in his granddaughter's third-grade class on Wednesdays. He was there from ten to three."

Wesley winked at the detective, as if to tell him he knew that too.

Lou couldn't get over the last bit of news, though. "I didn't realize either of them had any interest in editing the newspaper."

"Mitchell does," Sebastian said. "Robin? She just wants to be close to power, and she thinks I've got it."

Suddenly, Lou understood why Robin had acted so strange. It wasn't because she'd killed Godfrey, it was because Lou had mentioned Sebastian. The woman had a crush. The reason Robin had gone and bought Hermeowone in the first place became clear as well. Had Robin learned that Sebastian loved cats and tried to buy one to show him they had a similar interest, even though she knew nothing about cats?

"So Robin's out, and Mitchell's out," Noah summarized, having been fairly quiet during the conversation.

"Mitchell definitely seemed the least likely to be into nefarious dealings," Lou said. "So I'm glad to hear that it couldn't be him."

"So are we." Willow gestured between herself and Easton with her fork. "The man's been our neighbor for years. He loves to chat whenever we're out at the mailboxes."

Lou drew in a lungful of air. "Do you think he might give us information about the other two?"

Sebastian jabbed his fork toward Lou. "I like where your mind is going. Despite two being out, we could still be looking at one of the members of the BBS."

"He might talk." Willow turned toward Easton to get his opinion. When her significant other agreed, she said, "I can come by tomorrow and tell you what I know about him."

"You don't think he'll talk to you?" Noah asked, voicing one of the questions in Lou's mind.

Willow shook her head. "He knows I wouldn't keep

anything from Easton, and given the way the rest of the witnesses have been keeping things from him already in this case, I wouldn't want to chance it. I think it'll be better if Lou can get him to spill something on the younger two of the BBS members."

"From what I observed of Sasha and Adam throughout my tailing of Robin and Mitchell, they're capable of setting some fires to get what they need, if you know what I mean." Wesley widened his eyes for effect.

Sebastian leaned forward. "I'm wondering if you'll allow me to send Wesley into town to help. I'd love for him to hang out in Button. Maybe come help at the bookstore for a week or two, Lou." Sebastian speared a piece of broccoli and let it hang off the end of his fork as he waited for Lou's decision.

But Lou deferred to Easton. It wasn't her decision to make.

Easton, in the middle of chewing a bite, pondered the idea. Finally, he swallowed and said, "I think that might be a good idea. Wesley's proven to be a helpful set of eyes to have on the situation. He could be instrumental in helping us see something we might miss because we're locals."

George grumbled, "This week just got so much worse."

Wesley just smirked in her direction.

CHAPTER 13

As promised, Willow stopped by the next day to give Lou the lowdown on Mitchell Moore. Setting down her purse on the table in the bookshop, Willow dug through it, pulling out a pair of gardening gloves, a pair of scissors, and even a small branch before she found the piece of paper she was searching for.

"Okay," she said, squinting at the notes she'd taken. "Easton and I sat down last night after we got home and jotted down everything we know about the guy."

The bookshop was set to open in thirty minutes, so they would need to talk quickly. Willow also needed to make her way to the nursery. Though it didn't open as early as Whiskers and Words, Willow's opening work was a lot more time consuming than Lou's—which really just consisted of her feeding the cats, turning on her computer, and unlocking the front door.

"He drives the same brand of car as you do, Lou." Willow cringed at the first thing on the list, as if she hadn't realized how much of a stretch that one had been last night, but it was more than clear that it was a miss, in the moment. Her eyes lit up. "Oh, he loves books."

Lou and George shared a hopeful glance.

"Why haven't we ever seen him in here, then?" George scrunched up her nose.

Willow mirrored the facial expression. "Well, because, according to Easton, he's a staunch supporter of the local library."

Lou's heart felt heavier at the statement. She loved libraries as well. They were amazing institutions that did so much good in every community. But as a booklover, she also knew there were titles she wanted to keep forever, to display on her shelf so she could smile at them each time she passed by, remembering the parts of the story that stuck with her so long after she finished the last word. Did every reader silently hope a guest might wander over to their bookshelf and inquire about a certain book, giving the owner of said book the chance to gush about how much they loved it, recommend it, or maybe even loan it out? Sure. A reader's shelves were like odd trophy cases, displaying the worlds they'd visited and the emotions they'd felt so deeply when cradled in the soft, cream-colored pages. Shelves could also hold books a reader had yet to read. A full to-be-read shelf was a treasure Lou couldn't explain to someone who didn't already understand.

Willow snapped her fingers in front of Lou's face. "Where'd you go, Lou Lou?"

Flinching, Lou said, "Sorry, I—"

"Was just getting weird about books again. I know." Willow waved it off.

George chuckled.

"I think I can use his interest in books." Lou nodded resolutely.

"But he didn't even come to the community book swap you held this summer." George's expression tightened, leaving no room for hope. "Free books. Recycling. Promoting literacy. That event had it all, and he still didn't show. We might be dealing with someone who can't stand capitalism."

"And yet he used to own The Upholstered Button? No, I think I know what will work," Lou assured Willow. "Leave it to me. I'll figure it out."

Willow balked, dubious for a moment, but she stood and shoved everything back into her purse. "Okay, well, good luck."

Once Willow was gone, George asked, "What's the plan?"

"I'm going to show Mitchell Moore that I value libraries as much as he does. And I'm going to do it right in front of his house."

BACK WHEN LOU had purchased the bookstore, then Button Books, the previous owner had left a lot behind—including problems with some angry customers. One of the less-problematic leftovers was a Little Free Library. It must've been ordered straight from the company—if the small plaque denoting its authenticity on the front was anything to go by —and had been fully assembled. Instead of being installed somewhere outside the bookshop, however, Lou had found it propped in the corner of her office at the back of the shop.

She'd been meaning to do something with it for ages. Mitchell gave her the perfect excuse.

While installing a Little Free Library in the chilly November weather wasn't on the top of Lou's list of things she was comfortable with, at least it wasn't currently raining. She would have to take the small win.

It took a quick search of how-to videos online to make a list of the supplies she would need. After making a trip to the hardware store, Lou drove to Willow's house with the library in the back of her car. She parked close to the end of the driveway and focused her attention on the corner of Easton's property.

She'd texted him earlier, asking permission to install something by the road, letting him know she'd take it down immediately if he hated it. Easton had warily agreed. Lou hoped he would like it, but even if he didn't, the act of installing it should get Mitchell's attention.

For as cute as it was, the town of Button was sorely lacking when it came to the adorable fad of Little Free Libraries.

Putting one by Easton and Willow would mean anyone driving into town would see it, and it would be accessible by foot for both the Forest Pond neighborhood to the south and Noah's neighborhood on Pattern Drive to the north.

As Lou worked, she wondered if she should've gotten permission from the town before installing such a thing. Ironically, the person most likely to report her was already dead, so she supposed it didn't matter that she'd skipped that step.

She got stuck a few times, texting Noah specific questions about how deep to dig the hole before she poured the concrete inside and how long she would need to wait for it to dry. He answered all with very detailed instructions, but then, after her third question, he sent one follow-up text.

What are you up to?

She loved that she could hear the happiness in his voice even through the text message. Pulling out her phone, Lou snapped a picture of her progress and sent it back in response.

Did you ask Easton?

Noah must've recognized where she was.

Of course. Who do you think I am?

Someone who's very good at installing that library, except for those hinges. I'll be there to help you in thirty minutes when I'm done here.

She hadn't been the one to screw on the door, so that wasn't technically on her. Lou smiled to herself, the grin only growing when she noticed a man crossing the street from his house on the corner of Pattern Drive and Spool Avenue.

Mitchell.

He lifted his graying eyebrows in question as he approached. "Whatcha got going in here?" he asked.

Even though it was none of his business, since it wasn't anywhere near his property, Lou had expected as much. She was getting used to the people of Button and their nosy ways. And while in New York City, Lou might not have deigned to respond, this had been her plan all along.

"Oh, hi." She lifted a glove-clad hand. "I'm just installing a Little Free Library."

"But you own a bookstore." His tone held such conviction, as if the two couldn't possibly exist simultaneously.

Lou ducked her head. "Sure, and even though people buying books from me keeps me in business, I still like to support the free sharing of books. I don't know if you heard, but I did a book swap during the summer that was immensely popular. And it got me thinking of what else I could do to promote free book sharing within the community." She held her hand toward the library in progress.

Mitchell's scowl slowly loosened its grip over his features, the wrinkles on his face smoothing out somewhat as he relaxed.

"I'm going to donate books from the store to fill it initially." Lou gestured to the box of used books she'd brought with her. "But I hope that people will trade them for other books they don't need anymore." She rested on the shovel handle like it was a cane.

"That's … well, that's very … good." He nodded in appreciation and moved to walk away.

"Hey," she called out, stopping him. "You wouldn't know anything about how the hinges on this door should look, would you?"

Mitchell's lips eased from their tight, down-turned state. "Of course I do. Furniture is my business. Or, was." He seemed to stand straighter as he admitted that. When she cocked her head in question, he said, "I used to own The Upholstered Button, before I sold it to Bea." He lifted his chin with pride.

Even though she already knew that, the question seemed to soften him up. "Oh, that's great. I love that place. Bea furnished the sitting area in Whiskers and Words." She handed over the screwdriver when he motioned for it. She kept Noah's offer to help to herself, knowing any way she could buy more time with Mitchell by himself, the better.

"Sure." He was already rolling up the sleeves of his flannel shirt.

They got to work.

She sent the third nervous glance in his direction in as many minutes. "Can I ask you something, Mitchell?"

He grunted by way of an answer, so Lou took it as a yes.

"What happened at that last BBS meeting at Godfrey's house?" She hoped her look conveyed innocent intrigue rather than the interrogation she was actually doing.

Mitchell puffed out his cheeks and leaned on the shovel just as Lou had done earlier. "It was a mess."

For a split second, Lou thought he was going to leave it at that. But it turned out that Mitchell Moore was just as big of a gossip as Cricket, George, and Silas put together, because after that pause, everything came spilling out.

"Godfrey was in a *mood*." Mitchell cocked an eyebrow at Lou. "It all started before we got there. Brock Nolan was at his door when Sasha and I showed up. They were screaming at one another. But even after Nolan stomped off, and Robin and Adam showed up, Godfrey couldn't stop complaining about the noise from the construction and muttering about how Brock was ignoring his warnings. He said he was going to make him pay." Mitchell swiped at the sweat gathering on his forehead.

That would've been concerning if Lou, and the rest of Button, didn't already know that Brock had an alibi for Godfrey's time of death.

"Godfrey was so distracted that he knocked his drink onto the ground and it left a pink stain on the rug. He muttered that Diana was going to kill him as he sopped it up with a handkerchief." Mitchell sighed. "And then she called during the middle of the meeting. We tried not to listen, but she was yelling, and he only stepped into the kitchen, so we heard a lot more than we should've."

Well, that explained the stain she'd seen on the handkerchief, but not the words scribbled on after. A shiver ran over Lou's arms. When they'd been working, Lou's body heat had kept her warm enough, but now that they'd stopped, she realized what a sharp bite the November wind had to it.

"Like what?" Lou asked, running her hands up and down her goose-bump-covered arms. She checked over her shoulder, hoping Noah wouldn't show up in the middle of this monologue. As much as Mitchell seemed to open up to her, she wasn't sure he would keep talking with Noah there.

Mitchell wrinkled his nose. "I can't be sure, but it sounded like he'd been talking to a coffee chain about buying the Bean and Button from her. She'd gotten a call while she was out of town and wanted to know how dare he try to make her sell her business."

Lou gasped. Marital troubles alone didn't seem like a good enough motive. But if Godfrey had also been trying to sell her business… "So, he was actively working to bring a chain into Button?" The question wobbled as it came out of her mouth, and she suddenly wished Noah was already there.

Mitchell pinched his nose out of fatigue. "I'm not sure why it was such a surprise to the rest of them. We knew his focus was about control and the paint colors. It was never about big chains for him, like it was for us. We aligned ourselves with him because he was a means to an end."

Suddenly the conversation hadn't just shed light on a motive for Diana to kill Godfrey, but Mitchell had just given her confirmation that the BBS had a reason to want Godfrey dead as well. What if Sasha and Adam were mad enough about the coffee-chain conversation to get rid of him before the vote?

"Mitchell, did you all get together after that meeting, or did you go home?"

"We went our separate ways." He swallowed, as if he wished he'd stuck around a little longer.

But Lou worried if he had, he could've been collateral damage, because it sounded more and more likely that either one of the BBS members had taken him out or that Diana had tried to get revenge for Godfrey trying to sell her business out from under her. Peanut Butter had smelled her on the handkerchief that had been covering his face. Maybe Lou shouldn't have dismissed it so easily. It was possible the dog knew more than they did about the situation.

Lou gulped just as Noah pulled up in his truck.

CHAPTER 14

Mitchell glanced over Lou's shoulder. "It looks like your other help has arrived. I'll let you get to it." With a hand held up in a makeshift wave, he jogged across the street, back to his house.

Noah walked over, but just as he reached Lou, Easton pulled up. Lou pasted on a cheerful expression, studying Easton as he walked over, hoping he wouldn't be mad about what she'd done.

The detective eyed the library. "Oh good. I thought you were going to put up security cameras or something. This is much better."

Lou's lungs emptied quickly out of relief, glad he didn't mind.

"Did you find out anything from Mitchell?" Noah asked her.

Easton crossed his arms, intrigued.

"I did." Lou explained the meeting, from Mitchell's point of view, and the phone call with Diana.

Easton's gaze darkened. "Diana didn't tell me any of this."

"Of course she didn't," Lou said. "I wonder if she might've hired someone to kill her husband while she was out of town."

Easton's face paled. He swallowed hard.

"What is it?" Noah asked, his whole body seemed to stiffen.

"She didn't need to hire anyone," Easton said, his tone thin. "Because she wasn't in Vegas on the day Godfrey was killed."

Lou and Noah shared an amazed glance.

"She told me she got back the day after he died, but when I looked up her flight number, she wasn't on that plane. It took a little digging, but I found her on the previous day's flight home."

"She changed her flight to an earlier one, and then lied about it?" Lou asked.

Easton shook his head. "According to the airline, she booked that return flight from the beginning. She always knew she was coming back that day. I thought she just told me the wrong date and flight number because she was in shock, grieving, but now that we know she had a motive to kill Godfrey … I need to go talk to her." He shifted his feet as if he were itching to do that right then.

"If she lied about that, there has to be a reason." Noah's voice was strained.

"And it's probably not good." Lou cringed. "She could've been the person you saw in the Cranes' backyard that day when you were at Cricket's," Lou said, swatting toward Noah to bring him back from wherever his mind had disappeared to.

Eyes lighting up with recognition, proving Noah had told him about that as well, the detective stuffed his hands in his pockets. "I might go chat with Mitchell, just to get an official report of what he told you, Lou." He gestured to the blue house across the street.

Noah and Lou watched as he strode over to Mitchell's place, then they turned their attention back to the Little Free Library.

"He helped you with the door." Noah scratched at his beard.

Lou smiled. "Yeah." Her lips immediately dropped into a frown. "Are you okay with that? You seem upset that you didn't get to help me."

Noah raked his fingers through his hair.

"What's going on?" Lou asked softly, careful to keep her distance from him since they were standing out by the road, and anyone passing by could see if they touched.

Pain was clear in Noah's features. "All of this stuff about Godfrey and Diana's marriage just makes me think ... We need to tell Cassidy tonight."

Understanding smoothed over the worry that had built up rough patches in Lou's mind. Noah had grown increasingly agitated during the revelations about the Cranes' relationship.

"I know we're already divorced, but I never want to have that kind of secretive, antagonistic relationship with her. She's Marigold's mother." His arm flexed as he leaned down to pick up a screwdriver from the ground.

Lou wanted to come to his aid, to tell him not to be so hard on himself, to remind him that Cassidy had been secretive about the men she'd been dating, so it wasn't like they were doing anything different. But she knew he was right. Even when Cassidy had taken the low road, Noah would always take the high one.

She clapped her hands together. "Then let's do it. Let's tell her now."

CASSIDY LIVED in a beautiful little cottage off Ribbon Road. Because she was a real estate agent, and knowing the market was her job, she'd found a home she adored right after the divorce, letting Noah keep the house they'd lived in together.

And while Lou thought Noah's house was wonderful, Cassidy's was downright adorable. The exterior was a soft blue akin to the sky on a cloudless day. The light paint color of the house made the red door stand out even more, drawing one toward the entrance like a spell. The yard was a mixture of mature fruit trees, local wildflowers, and a few vegetable beds. The woman Cassidy had bought the place from had been a master gardener, and Cass did her best to maintain the beautiful space the former owner had cultivated.

Cassidy met them on the porch, worrying creasing her forehead. Noah had texted on the way, giving her a heads-up, but he'd simply said he needed to talk to her, so she was still in the dark about the subject of the chat.

"Everything's okay," Noah said as they approached. Cassidy checked her watch, prompting Noah to add, "I know you have to get Goldie in less than an hour."

Cass's eyes contracted a bit before she gestured to the love seat and two Adirondack chairs on the covered porch. She settled back into one of the chairs, body tense in anticipation, despite the low, laid-back way the chair forced her to sit.

Noah pulled a deep breath in through his nose. "I wanted to let you know that Lou and I are—"

"Dating?" Cassidy blurted out, interrupting him mid-sentence.

Lou tensed as Noah nodded, and they waited for Cassidy to follow that outburst with reasons she thought it was a bad idea.

"Thank goodness," she said, collapsing back into the chair in relief.

Noah and Lou shared a confused glance, but it was tinged with a grin.

Cassidy tilted her head and shot them a serious stare. "I've been hoping the two of you would figure it out for a while now."

"You're not upset?" Lou wet her lips.

"Upset? I'm thrilled." Cassidy's blue eyes locked on to her as palpably as if she'd reached out her hand and grabbed on to Lou's. "I mean, Noah can date whoever he wants. But, given that whoever's in his life is also going to be in Marigold's, I'm selfishly glad it's you."

Lou's heart felt like it fluttered with happiness, and tears stung at her eyes.

Cass sat forward again. "What did Goldie say?"

"We haven't told her yet," Noah explained. "We wanted to tell you first, and initially we were waiting to see what this was before pulling Goldie into it."

Cassidy's face broke into a warm smile as she stared at Noah. "Initially?"

Noah cleared his throat, the sound moving into a chuckle. "I don't want to speak for Lou, but it didn't take me long to realize that it was always going to be long term for me." He checked with Lou.

Her cheeks warmed, sharing his feeling. "We've kinda been enjoying sneaking around for a while. You know Button."

Rolling her eyes at the nosy town, Cass said, "Well, I think it was smart to wait. It's what I should've done."

Noah stayed silent. It was no secret to either Cassidy or Lou that Noah wished Cass had waited a little longer before she'd introduced the guy she was seeing to Marigold.

"Luckily, Greg wasn't as big a part of Marigold's life. Not like Lou is." The woman appraised Lou with such warmth, she couldn't help but feel sure that she had Cassidy's blessing.

"But it's getting complicated, and we think it might be for the best to come clean." Lou winced, remembering the hurt Noah had endured over the past week just to keep the secret.

Cassidy frowned in question.

"Godfrey Crane's body. I didn't find him by myself. Lou was with me," Noah explained. "But without a reason I would've been in the woods with her, we kept that fact from everyone but Easton."

"Why *were* you in the woods with her?" Cassidy asked with a chuckle.

Lou wrinkled her nose. "George is living with me right now…"

Cassidy's expression glimmered with understanding. "Ah, and you needed to get out of the apartment, away from prying eyes. Gotcha."

"We hadn't told you yet, and I didn't want the rest of the town to find out before you." Noah looked at his hands.

All understanding left her expression as she seemed to contemplate that. "Noah, you let people believe all of that terrible stuff about you just because you hadn't told me yet?" Now it seemed like it was Cassidy's turn to tear up. She glanced up at the wooden slats along the porch ceiling. "I'm so sorry I didn't give you the same courtesy."

Noah smiled kindly. "It's okay, Cass. We're all just figuring this out as we go."

Sniffing, Cass checked her watch, swiping her fingers under her eyes. "I should head out to grab Marigold soon."

The three of them stood.

"Unless you want her tonight so you can tell her the good news," Cassidy offered. But before Noah could answer, she snapped her fingers. "Actually, she's got the science fair this Friday and only *just* started that project. Maybe wait until after she turns it in so she doesn't lose focus?"

"We can do that," Noah said. "This weekend sounds great."

Cassidy pulled them each into a hug, repeating her congratulations and thanking them again for letting her know first.

Lou's heart felt as if it might burst from happiness. When she'd first moved to town, she'd taken the close nature of Cassidy and Noah's divorced relationship as evidence that maybe they weren't over, that they might mend things and get back together. But what she realized over time was that even if they weren't romantically interested in each other anymore, they'd known one another most of their lives and were great friends. Noah's insistence on keeping his relationship with Cassidy strong and healthy for his daughter's sake was only one of the things that had made Lou fall for him.

Once they were back in Noah's truck, Lou let out a long sigh. Noah rubbed a hand over his face. They gazed at one another, twin smiles mirrored perfectly on their faces. Noah drove back to Willow's so Lou could get her car. Once they were parked in Willow's driveway, Noah's elation seemed to take over his whole body, and as the minutes went by, the excitement over Cassidy's reaction only seemed to increase.

"Want to go out to dinner with me?" Noah asked, his dark eyes alight.

Lou let out a weightless laugh. "Hold on, there. We haven't told Marigold yet. You know, if the town sees us having dinner, they're going to talk. That'll definitely distract her from the science fair."

And the local kids were just as good at spreading gossip as their parents. Marigold often surprised them with the amount she knew, just having overheard bits of information in school.

Flinching momentarily, Noah said, "True. What about Brine? No one knows us over there."

Lou thought about the quirky pickle-themed town next door, a grin slowly spreading over her face. Willow and many other Buttonites might grumble about their neighbor, but Lou had always found the place to be charming and fun. "Okay. Yes. Let's do it."

The slight incline of Noah's head made it seem like he might lean over to kiss her before stopping himself. Even though the sneaking around had been kind of fun, now that having their secret out in the open was within reach, she couldn't wait to kiss him in public, without worrying about who might see.

Lou's gaze settled on the finished Little Free Library on Easton's property. "I need to stop by the store first to check in with George, but then I'll meet you out there."

Noah's dimples deepened. "Unless you feel like pizza, the only other option is the diner."

Lou had never been to the In a Pickle diner, but she'd thoroughly enjoyed going to the Salty Slice with her nieces last summer when they visited. And while Button often felt so small to her, the fact that they had the bistro, the barbecue place, and a pizza joint made it feel decadent and full of choices.

"Let's do the Salty Slice." Lou dipped her chin resolutely.

He squeezed her hand, and they parted ways.

But when Lou arrived at the bookstore, George was gone. She'd left a note on the interior side of the back door.

Lou, had to get out for a bit. Wesley hung out at the shop for most of the day today, and he used up all my patience. See you later tonight.

Oh no. Lou had forgotten about Sebastian sending Wesley to the bookshop. He hadn't specified what day that would begin, but she wouldn't have left George alone with the guy if she'd known.

With George gone, Lou didn't bother going upstairs. She returned to her car and drove toward Brine. Noah waited at a table in the front of the restaurant, wearing a smile as big as the pizzas the servers were sliding onto tables.

"George okay?" he asked as she scooted into the seat across from him.

"I think so. She wasn't there. Said she needed to get out. It was Wesley, though, not anything bad."

"Ah, Wesley." Noah's dark eyes gleamed with a teasing grin. "I can't figure the two of them out."

"I can," Lou scoffed. "They hate each other."

Noah inclined his head like he was going to say something more, but their server approached.

They'd just ordered a pizza, and the server had brought out their drinks when—

"Lou? Noah?"

Lou's spine straightened at the sound of George's voice. She and Noah turned to see George and Brynn walking through, toward an empty table. George's attention narrowed in on the two of them.

"What are you doing here?"

They'd been caught.

CHAPTER 15

Lou gaped at George and Brynn for a moment before she laughed awkwardly. "What are we doing here?" She repeated the question. "We're having dinner. Installing that library made me hungry," she said, as if they came there all the time.

George's pupils contracted as her gaze flicked between Lou and Noah.

"Why would you come here instead of going to Slice of Button?" She crossed her arms.

Brynn shifted her feet in discomfort.

"Because you know who owns the place in Button, and we didn't want to chance a run-in," Lou said as the idea came to her. Relief filled her as George seemed to buy the story. "Especially after what we learned today."

Leaning toward Brynn, George said, "Sasha owns the pizza place by us, and she's part of that group I was telling you about." She turned to Lou. "What did you learn today?"

"Only that Godfrey might not have been so supportive of their efforts to keep big businesses out of Button," Lou said. "But Sasha is still second to Diana, who moved up to our top suspect."

George and Brynn shared a glance filled with intrigue. Brynn may not have been from Button, but she was a small-towner from Brine and liked gossip as much as her neighbors.

"What are *you* doing here?" Lou asked, trying to turn the question back on her friend, even though it was fairly clear that she was just meeting Brynn for dinner.

Ever since they'd mildly accused Brynn's father of murder during the spring, they'd all become good friends, but none so much as George and Brynn. While George was an old soul and loved the older residents of Button, she was a young woman in her twenties. Meeting Brynn, who also shared in George's love of online gaming, had meant George finally had someone else her age to hang out with.

To Lou's surprise, however, George seemed flustered to have her own question turned back on her. Her cheeks flushed pink, and her gaze flitted around the restaurant as if she didn't want to tell Lou why they were there.

Noah must've been so surprised about seeing people they knew out and about that he didn't seem to notice George's odd behavior, but Lou's detail-oriented mind clocked every move.

"Brynn and I are just hanging," George blurted. Then, without asking, she took one of the two empty seats at Noah and Lou's table. Her cheeks turned even redder as she glanced up at them. "Do you mind if we join you two?" she asked, finally remembering her manners.

It was Lou's turn to feel heat splash across her face. There wasn't a good reason they shouldn't have company, if they were just friends, like George thought. Noah grabbed Lou's hand under the table and squeezed.

Meeting Noah's eyes, Lou saw him nod, ever so slightly. He was telling her it was okay, that they could tell George. She could keep a secret for a few days while they waited to tell Marigold. Relief filled Lou.

But before she could even open her mouth to spill the secret, someone placed a hand on her shoulder. She jumped, turning to see Wesley Saint James pulling up a fifth chair.

"Hey," he said, his floppy blond hair falling into his face as he surveyed the table. "You all taking a break for sustenance too? Right on."

"A break from what?" Noah asked.

Wesley scoffed, "From the Godfrey case."

"You're investigating in Brine?" Lou asked. "I thought Sebastian wanted you to hang around Button."

Snorting, Wesley shook his head. "I live here, remember? I'm just coming back into town after a very informative day in Button, spent with my favorite lady." He winked at George, reminding Lou of the note she'd left about Wesley's presence in the shop that day.

George groaned and pulled a face.

Caught up, Lou said, "Uh, yeah. We found out some pretty big stuff today too."

"Mi information es su information," Wesley said in broken Spanish. "Who wants to go first?" He looked from Lou to Noah to George.

George rolled her eyes. "Don't look at me. You were literally in my hair all day. We know the same things." Lou could've sworn George muttered something after, but she couldn't quite make out what it was.

The server showed with the pizza Noah and Lou ordered, and they all dug in, ordering a second one with different toppings since the number at their table had more than doubled.

"Okay, well, I learned that Godfrey's wife, Diana, found out that he was talking to coffee chains about selling the Bean and Button," Lou said after swallowing her first bite.

"Out from under her?" George asked, appalled.

"We don't know," Noah answered for Lou. "But it could give her motive to get him out of the way, especially if they put his name on the business when they got married and he had an equal share of the coffeehouse."

Lou peered over her shoulder and leaned closer before saying, "And Easton found out that she wasn't on the flight she said she was on. She flew in the day before." Given how open Easton had been to sharing information with the private investigator during their dinner at Sebastian's, Lou didn't think he would mind her sharing that piece of information with Wesley.

"So she was in town when her husband was killed after all," Brynn summarized, disbelief lightening her tone.

Wesley swallowed and sat back. "Oh man. That's big.

And here I thought what *I'd* learned was going to be the thing that would split this case wide open."

Lou and Noah exchanged an excited glance.

"What did you learn?" Lou asked.

Wesley held up a finger as he chewed a bite of pizza and then swallowed. "I chatted with the construction guys today."

"From the old Rossback mansion?" Noah asked, then amended that, saying, "Nolan mansion, now, I suppose."

"The very same." Wes set down the slice of pizza.

"But they told Easton they didn't see anything." Lou chewed on her bottom lip.

Smiling slyly, Wesley said, "You'd be surprised how much guys open up when you bring them free sandwiches and sodas for lunch." He leaned back in a gesture of self-satisfaction.

George circled her hand in the air, obviously having heard the story already. "Get to the point."

"I asked them if they saw anyone else approach the house after the BBS members left," Wesley explained. "And they told me one of them didn't leave right away."

Noah's forehead wrinkled in question, and Lou gripped the table.

"Who?" she asked.

"They called her the younger woman, and we know it wasn't Robin since I started following her right after that, so I'm guessing they were talking about Sasha." Wesley's eyes sparkled with the information.

"Sasha went back to talk to Godfrey," Lou repeated, as if

saying it aloud might help it seem real. "To fight with him about something?" she wondered.

"He's not even telling you the most important part," George scoffed. "Sasha didn't go to the front door. She skirted around the back of the house."

"I saw a woman with brown hair in the Cranes' back-yard, and Godfrey was on his back deck when I found him," Noah said, just above a whisper.

Lou swallowed. "He might've stopped answering the door with his gun at the ready, but he definitely would've grabbed it if he heard someone trying to get into his house through the back door."

"But then, that means Diana lied for nothing about coming back on an earlier flight," Brynn observed.

Wesley took a bite of his crust, lifting one shoulder. "The construction crew said they didn't see anyone else show up after that, so maybe Diana had something else going on."

Lou took a long gulp of water, hoping it would help the lump in her throat. "Wesley, you have to tell this to Easton as soon as you can."

Wesley dipped his head in understanding. "I figured I'd stop by tomorrow morning before I head to the bookshop."

"Oh, joy," George grumbled.

"You didn't seem to hate me so much when I brought *you* a sandwich, too, after I met with the construction crew." Wesley watched her as if daring her to lie.

She merely turned her attention to her drink, focusing on taking another sip.

"I can hold down the bookshop tomorrow, if you want a break," Lou offered.

George coughed, her eyes watering a little as some of her drink went into her airway. Swiping at them, George said, "It's okay. I don't want to leave you alone."

Lou couldn't help but wonder why her friend's cheeks turned red. Was it really just a reaction from her drinking misstep, or was something else going on?

CHAPTER 16

The next morning, Lou was just settling onto the stool behind the register counter with her second cup of coffee when Willow called. Wesley must've still been talking to Easton at the station, because he hadn't shown up yet, much to the delight of George. Lou eyed her warily, still wondering about her behavior last night, as she answered Willow's call.

"Hello?" Lou glanced out at the rain spattering down on the fall streets, littered with colorful leaves from the surrounding trees.

"Hey." Willow's voice was rushed with excitement. "Someone just pulled up to the Little Free Library."

Lou placed a hand on her hip. "Are you spying on them from your front window like a creeper?"

"I have nothing better to do. It's my day off, and it's raining too hard to ride or work in the garden." Her tone flattened into a pout.

A low, baying bark sounded in the background, making Lou jump at the sound.

"Peanut Butter," Willow snapped. "Shhhh. Now they definitely know we're watching them."

"Peanut Butter?" Lou asked.

"Brenner had to leave town for his brother's wedding. Apparently, it's a multiday affair. Easton was going to take him to work with him, but the big guy looked so sad about the thought of going out in the rain that I said he could stay here with me and cuddle on the couch while I read. Except, I'm wishing I hadn't offered now." Her tone turned into more of a hiss. "Okay, the people are gone. Should we go see what book they took, PB?" she asked.

Lou wondered why she was even still on the call if Willow was just going to talk to the dog instead of her. But she was rather interested in the book that had been taken as well, so she stayed on the line while Willow slipped on her rubber boots, clipped Peanut Butter to his leash, and unfurled her umbrella to go out into the rain.

While she listened to the hilarious commentary of her best friend as she completed those steps, George wandered down from upstairs, waving good morning to Lou. Geralt trotted at her heels, staring longingly at the baby wrap she usually wore him in draped over one shoulder. She frowned at the phone as if to ask who it was, so Lou mouthed "Willow." George yawned as she began twisting the cotton wrap around her body in the crisscross pattern that would effectively hold the large cat.

On the other end of the call with Willow, the sound of

soggy footsteps rang through the line, sloshing as she walked down the driveway.

"Aww, Peanut Butter," Willow complained. "Don't pee *there*." She groaned. "I'm afraid the big guy just christened the stand for your library, friend. Sorry."

Lou chuckled. "I'm sure he won't be the last dog that pees on it. Don't worry about it."

"Okay, let's see…" Willow left the sentence hanging as she opened the door with a squeak. Lou reminded herself to grease the hinges next time she was there.

"How's the roof holding up in the rain? Any leaks?" Lou held her breath as she waited. She hadn't built the thing, just installed it, so she didn't know how sound it was.

Willow clicked her tongue. "Looks good. No leaks, so far."

Exhaling, Lou listened while, from the muffled sounds coming through the phone, Willow repositioned the phone and started searching through the books inside.

"Any clue what they took? Or if they left anything?" Lou asked impatiently.

There was a small gasp on Willow's end. Or had that been the sound of a car passing by on the wet roadway?

"Willow?" Lou asked, concern growing.

Her tone must've changed because George snapped her head toward Lou just as she got Geralt settled in his wrap. She stalked over to the register where Lou sat, furrows in her forehead deepening with each step forward.

"Uh, Lou," Willow finally said.

Was it just Lou, or was her best friend's voice shaking?

"I think you need to get over here." Willow's gulp after that was so loud, Lou heard it clearly on her end.

"What?" She stood but kept the phone pressed to her ear.

"Someone left a book, all right, but it has a note inside, a note about Godfrey." Peanut Butter let out that same baying bark in the background. "Actually, I'm texting Easton too. Both of you need to see this."

George must've heard the intensity in Lou's voice because she waved her toward the back, nonverbally telling her she'd watch the bookshop.

EASTON WAS JUST GETTING out of his car when Lou pulled up to Willow's. They shared a dark look as they arrived on the porch, both shivering from the short sprints they had to do through the pelting rain.

Willow hadn't even gone inside. She was sitting, rocking chaotically in a chair on her porch. Peanut Butter's bays could still be heard from inside. She flinched each time the dog started up again.

"He won't stop," she complained as Easton and Lou jogged up the front steps. "He just kept pawing at me and barking.

Easton's mouth was a grim line, but he opened the front door and called a gentle, "Well done, Peanut Butter. Off duty."

Immediately, the dog quieted. Easton closed the door, leaving the canine inside as he came over to Willow. Lou was already kneeling next to her friend, trying to glean whatever information she could from her expression.

"Sorry about Peanut Butter," Easton said, placing a hand on her arm. "I didn't think you'd need to know his release phrase since he wasn't on duty today."

"Does he often go off like that?" Lou knew the dog was on the younger side. Both he and Brenner were less than a year out of graduating from their respective academies, but he seemed so proficient every other time she'd interacted with him.

"No." Easton's lips twitched. "And if Willow didn't give him a new command, him barking like that means that he caught a scent he'd already been given."

Lou's eyes widened and flashed up to Easton's. "The handkerchief," she said, barely above a whisper. They settled on the note in Willow's hands.

"That's all going to make so much more sense when you see what's on this note." She held it toward them, wincing. "Sorry, I touched it before I realized it was a clue."

Easton didn't take the note, not having gloves on either and not wanting to add more fingerprints to the thing, but simply let Willow hold it as they read.

It wasn't a long note. Lou wasn't sure what she'd expected ,but it *definitely* wasn't what was written there.

I'm the one who killed Godfrey, but not for the reason you think.

Lou blinked at the words, typed on a computer and printed out so they wouldn't be able to trace anything back with handwriting.

"Why would the killer tell us this?" Lou asked, Willow's porch feeling suddenly unsteady. She glanced at the book that the note had been stuck inside. It was *The Company Man* by W. H. Whyte. At the moment, all she could remember about the title was that it had been published sometime around the mid-twentieth century and that it felt familiar, but she couldn't place why.

Easton took a different tack. "Do you remember anything about the car that dropped off the book?"

"I've been trying to remember every detail I could," Willow said. "I didn't catch the license plate, but I remember that it was a red sedan, and the back left brake light was broken, like, the plastic had a hole in it because white light shone through the red."

"I can work with that." Easton jotted down that information. He held up a finger, moving inside. When he came back, he wore rubber gloves, and held out his hand for the book.

Willow placed the note back inside the book and handed them both over at once.

Staring at the book, Lou recognized why it sounded familiar to her. "Ben used that book—well, excerpts from it —during his course on capitalism in literature. That unit was filled with stuff like *Atlas Shrugged*. Unlike Rand, Whyte argued that there needed to be a balance between the corporation and the individual, that a man's obligation is in the *here and now*," she said, repeating one of the phrases from the book she remembered Ben going over and over in his notes.

"What did Rand think?" Willow narrowed her eyes.

"I might be getting this wrong," Lou said, closing one eye. "It's been a while. But I think she argued that 'rational selfishness' was the key to thriving, and she defends the freedom of a man's mind," Lou explained.

Easton tilted his head. "The BBS and their proposition would've definitely been a breach of individualism, opting more for the conformity needed to become part of a corporation. How is that different from what we thought?" he asked, motioning to the note left in the book. "We've always wondered if his involvement with the BBS was the motive behind his death. The handkerchief over his face said *Stop the Vote* after all."

"It could be Sasha," Lou said, checking with Easton. "I'm guessing you talked to Wesley."

"I have an officer speaking to the construction crew as we speak. If we can get them to verify what they told Wesley, Sasha moves up as our top suspect." Easton's forehead wrinkled in confusion. "Why would she want to stop the vote?"

"Because she guessed they didn't have enough support yet? And maybe Godfrey was pushing it forward, trying to make sure it was on the next ballot?" Even as Lou said it, the motivation didn't seem to be there, especially since the remaining members of the BBS had admitted that getting on the next ballot had been their goal as well.

Frustration pinpricked through Lou's brain as it tried to work out what the note could mean, but her brain felt foggy. In fact, a headache had been brewing since earlier that morning.

Easton lifted the bag. "I'd better get this back to the station."

The women waved goodbye as Easton left.

"You okay?" Willow asked Lou once Easton had returned to his car. "Your face is all scrunched in pain."

Lou relaxed her forehead, which had been furrowed. "I've just had a headache all morning." She inhaled through her nose, letting the crisp fall air wash into her nostrils. It felt as if it washed over her aching brain. "But the fresh air is making it better."

"Want to go on a walk before you return to the shop?" Willow glanced behind Lou, prompting her to do the same. "I've been waiting for a break in the rain to take Peanut Butter on a proper walk."

It had, in fact, stopped raining.

"Sure." Lou shoved her hands into her pockets.

Willow went inside to grab Peanut Butter, and they set off, crossing the road to the Forest Pond neighborhood, where there were sidewalks. The dog definitely knew he wasn't with his owner and handler, because he sniffed at just about every blade of grass and pulled Willow this way and that. She just rolled her eyes and turned her attention toward Lou.

"How are you doing with having George stay with you?" she asked.

Lou bobbed her head. "It's amazing. She's been so helpful and is watching the place for me a ton." She opened her palms and gestured to the two of them. "Like, right now."

"But…" Willow dragged out the word, showing that she could read Lou better than anyone.

A hint of a smile swept across Lou's face as she was reminded how much she loved her friend. "But … I feel bad not telling her. She's one of my closest friends, and even if the rest of Button doesn't know, shouldn't she?"

"But it's not your choice, right? Marigold is Noah's daughter, and both he and Cass decided it would be better if you waited to tell her. George will understand that," Willow said.

As if he were agreeing with Willow, Peanut Butter let out a low baying bark. He sat right in the middle of the sidewalk.

Glancing up, Lou realized that they'd just passed by Godfrey Crane's house.

"Okay, Peanut Butter," Willow said forcefully. "Good job. Yes, that's where the crime happened. You're off duty, though, Buddy." The dog panted up at her and wagged his tail as he stood. Looking at Lou, Willow said, "Easton told me this kind of thing is pretty common with younger dogs. He'll grow out of most of this impulsiveness."

Lou patted his head as they continued their walk but couldn't help but wonder if the reason Peanut Butter was so interested in the Crane house wasn't because of Godfrey, but Diana.

"Back to your George problem," Willow said. "You're going to tell Marigold soon, right?"

Lou nodded.

"Well, then you'll tell George soon. She'll understand. She might thank you since she's a terrible liar, and you're saving her from having to keep a secret."

"Yeah. You're right."

"I usually am." Willow winked at her.

Lou ran her shoulder into her friend. "How are *you* doing? I've been so consumed with my secret relationship, I haven't even checked in on you lately."

A soft smile overtook Willow's features. "I'm good. The nursery's great. Easton and I are fantastic." But her cheerful expression disappeared. "Oh, but we *are* having a bit of a dilemma."

Lou raised her eyebrows in question.

"We're thinking of moving in together." Willow curled her lips in to keep her grin semi-contained.

Eyes wide, Lou gasped. "Willow, that's wonderful."

"Thanks." Willow beamed. "But we're not sure what to do with Easton's house."

Lou didn't even need to ask why they would choose one house over the other. While they were both nice, Willow's home was, well, more of a home. Easton's house was much sparser, with fewer personal touches, and would be a lot easier to sell or rent. Not to mention Willow's house held the garden she'd spent a decade cultivating, as well as the barn and arena out back for O.C. and Steve.

"We could sell it, but Easton's convinced having an income property might be even better in the long term." She rolled her eyes as if she was replaying a conversation they'd had about it lately, one of many.

Lou patted her arm. "You two will figure it out. I hope

whoever moves in doesn't mind the Little Free Library I just installed in front of the house, though. Sorry. I didn't realize you two were thinking of moving in together when I put that in."

Willow waved off Lou's worries. "If they don't like libraries, we don't want 'em." She wrapped an arm around Lou's shoulders, and they walked back toward her house.

CHAPTER 17

While the fresh air helped with Lou's headache, it was short lived. By the time Lou arrived back at the bookshop, her headache had moved into her sinuses and her nose had become stuffed. She sniffed and let out a groan.

"I think you caught something while you were working outside yesterday." George wrinkled her nose as she surveyed her.

It *had* been colder than she'd expected, especially once she'd stopped moving around and started talking to Mitchell. Lou stopped to say hello to Sapphire, where he was curled up in a ball on the stack of books on the front table. Sinking her fingers into his soft fur, she let her eyelids flutter closed for a moment.

"I feel like I could sleep for days."

George jerked her thumb toward the back staircase. "You should. I've got it covered around here."

"Are you sure?" Lou hated to ask her to do so, but she

had to admit, the timing was great since George was around. She normally would've had to close if she got sick.

George held up a finger. "Just stay down here a few more minutes, if you can." She grabbed her purse from under the register and slung it across her body. "I'm going to have Ruby make you some of that immunity tea she has. It's got all those great medicinal herbs. If you drink some of that and then sleep, I'd bet you'll be feeling better in no time."

Lou waved in thanks as George disappeared out the door, jogging across the street toward the Bean and Button. She returned only a minute later, hands empty of tea.

"Ruby was out?" Lou guessed.

But George shook her head. "She was a little slammed at the moment, so she said she'd bring it over in a few minutes."

Lou spent the time shelving a few books while she waited. About five minutes later, Ruby crossed the street, a to-go cup of steaming hot tea balanced in front of her. Lou met her at the door, sure the woman would only be able to drop off the drink before returning to the coffeehouse. But Ruby stepped inside, letting the door close behind her.

She must've read the confusion on Lou's face because she said, "I wanted to come over here because I have something to ask you."

Lou wrapped her hands around the warm cup, gesturing to the table where they could sit. George joined them.

Ruby glanced over her shoulder, but George said, "It's just the three of us in here."

Geralt let out a low meow.

"Well, us and the cats." George gave Geralt a pointed scowl. "I wore you all morning. You can be on the ground a little while longer."

They turned their attention back to Ruby. The woman swallowed before looking at Lou. "I need some advice. I'm not sure if I'm freaking out for nothing, or…"

Lou nodded warily, willing Ruby to finish that thought.

"I was in the office today, and I saw something interesting." Ruby checked over her shoulder as if someone might be standing right there. "Diana left her phone on my desk, and I saw a calendar notification pop up for tomorrow night. It said *Sales Meeting*."

Lou and George exchanged a questioning glance.

"And there's no chance that's just a Bean and Button sales meeting you're not invited to?" George asked.

"Nope. I run those, and we have them on the last Saturday of each month."

"I *may* know what that's about," Lou said, hoping Easton wouldn't mind her telling Ruby. But the woman deserved to know. If Diana sold, it was unlikely that Ruby would be able to keep her job. So, she explained what Mitchell had told her about the phone call Godfrey received from Diana during the final BBS meeting at the Cranes'.

"But if she was so mad at Godfrey for talking with the big chains, why would she take a meeting with one of them?" George's mouth pulled into a tight line.

Lou twitched her shoulders. "Maybe Diana wasn't as mad about the idea of selling as we assumed. Maybe the idea grew on her, and she decided to take the meeting anyway."

"You think she's going to sell to one of the big chains after all?" Ruby asked, her tone tight. She let her head fall forward in defeat. "That's what I was afraid of. I've been very clear with her that I want to buy the business, so I'm not sure why she would consider anyone else. Unless she believes she can get more money through a chain." The realization seemed to rock Ruby's confidence.

Which, in turn, rocked Lou's. Ruby was not only self-assured, but she backed it up by being very good at what she did. She loved running the Bean and Button and had often commiserated with Lou, and Lindsey, the owner of the bakery across the street, that she was envious of them owning their businesses, that she wished she owned the coffeehouse.

The coffee shop manager swallowed. "I can't follow her. She'll recognize me, for sure." Ruby squinted one eye at Lou. "I was thinking she might not be as quick to recognize you, though. Will you follow her tomorrow night, and let me know who she meets with?"

Despite the fogginess in Lou's cold-addled brain, she said, "Of course."

"Thank you," Ruby said with a wave. "The meeting is at six, but I'm not sure where. She's staying late tomorrow to help me with inventory, so I'll text you when she leaves, and you can follow her."

A gust of wind entered as Ruby exited. Leaves skittered by the window, a few of the colorful oak leaves falling as if to join in on the race down the street. Lou shivered and took a sip of the tea, which had thankfully cooled slightly while they talked.

"Okay, now I'm going to sleep." Lou closed her eyes as she savored the hot tea.

When she opened her eyes, George was making a face that looked part smile, part cringe. "Feel better," she said.

Lou staggered upstairs, taking some cold medicine and then curling up on the couch. She didn't have the strength to change out of her outside clothes and didn't want to get in her bed with those on, so she opted for the soft couch, pulling a blanket off the back to cover her. She sent a quick message to Noah, letting him know she wasn't feeling well and was going to nap for a while.

The last thing she remembered seeing before her eyes slid shut was Hermeowone Granger, sitting across the room, staring at her.

Lou woke to the pinging sound of her phone's text message alert. She snapped her eyes open, groping at the coffee table next to the couch where she left the thing.

She expected to see a text from Noah, checking in on her after she'd messaged earlier. But the most recent text wasn't from Noah. It was from George.

Don't move. Look at your legs.

Lou blinked at the message. Panic coursed through her. Why couldn't she move?

Her gaze cutting over to the entrance to the apartment, Lou caught George standing there, frozen. But the look on her face wasn't of fear. It was awe, maybe even a little surprise. So Lou looked at her feet, and her lips parted.

The small, gray cat who had hissed and hid all week was tucked into a ball on the extra section of blanket past her feet. And while the cat wasn't technically touching Lou, the fact that it had even come that close felt like the biggest win.

"Apparently, she feels sorry for me," Lou whispered, sounding even more stuffed up than she had before she'd taken a nap.

George chuckled quietly and walked into the kitchen. "Do you want me to grab something from the bistro for you for dinner?"

Lou's heart swelled. It was a lovely offer, one Noah had made via text while she'd been sleeping—now that she checked her messages. But she shook her head. "I doubt I'll be able to taste much. I think I have some ramen noodles in the pantry. I might just make those."

"I've got it." George flapped a hand toward her to stop her from getting up.

She sank back into the pillow. Relief—or, as much as she could feel in her state—settled over her. Responding to Noah, she let him know George was taking care of her and she would call him in the morning.

They found *Fantastic Mr. Fox* playing on the television and let its fall vibes seep into the cozy apartment while they ate their soup. Hermeowone stayed curled up next to Lou the whole night.

CHAPTER 18

Unfortunately, Lou felt even worse when she woke up than she had the night before. Her head pulsed with a sinus headache, and she was pretty sure she was running a fever.

George's face tightened with obvious sympathy the moment Lou stumbled into the kitchen. "That's it. You're taking today off. I can run the shop. I've only got two tech appointments, and they're both coming to me."

Gratefulness surged through Lou. "Thank you. I really appreciate it." She blew her nose, hoping that would make it easier to get words out without feeling like she was pinching her nose. "I'm going to have to tell Ruby I can't follow Diana for her tonight." Lou shook her head, regretting the motion immediately as it caused her brain to throb with pain.

"I can do it." George's eyes flashed with excitement. "Diana doesn't know me all that well either."

Lou frowned. How could that be? Everyone in town knew George, it seemed.

"I don't drink a lot of coffee," she said.

"Okay. But make sure you stay safe."

George saluted. The promise of excitement later seemed to give her a kick of energy, because she said, "I'm going to run out and grab breakfast before I open, then. Want anything?"

Almost shaking her head again, Lou thought better of it. Then, because she hadn't already said no, she changed her mind about breakfast. "One of those morning glory muffins from the bakery would be great, actually." They at least had bran and carrot, along with other goodies that would taste great and fill her stomach so she wouldn't have to eat much until another soup lunch.

With the order taken, George was off. Lou eyed Hermeowone who was sleeping on the couch. As if she could feel Lou's attention on her, the little gray-and-white cat peeked open one eye.

"You're going to have a buddy today, I'm afraid." Lou sniffed, padding into the kitchen to start coffee, not sure if she would even be able to taste it due to how congested she was.

The cat blinked but went back to sleep.

And that was pretty much where they both stayed for the majority of the day. Lou alternated between reading, napping, and drinking tea, sticking to her end of the couch while Hermeowone stayed on the other.

Noah brought her soup at lunch, having ventured to the Vietnamese restaurant in Silver Lake to grab her favorite pho, the perfect comfort meal. Fixing a bowl of the soup for her, he set it on the coffee table before kneeling next to the couch. He placed the back of his hand to her forehead before letting his rough fingers trail down her cheek.

"It feels like your fever is down, at least." He flinched as his eyes met hers.

The care in his expression made the ache in her bones ease. She covered his hand with hers.

"Willow asked you to bring me soup if George asks." She winked at him. "I'll send her a text."

"I hate to run, but I've got a client coming in ten minutes." Leaning forward, Noah kissed her forehead.

"Thank you." She let her eyes slide closed for a moment, savoring the way Noah smelled like aftershave and the soap from his veterinary clinic.

He stood. "I'll check in later."

Once Noah was gone, Lou texted Willow so she'd be in on the story about the soup. She got a thumbs-up in response from her best friend just as she slurped away at the delicious meal. After eating, she took more cold medicine and fell into another nap.

It was dark outside once Lou woke once more. Worry grabbed at her throat with the thought that she might've missed Ruby's text about Diana leaving for the night, but she still had an hour until Diana's meeting. Setting her phone next to her on the couch, Lou took out her book and read until George came up after closing the shop.

But George wasn't alone. Anne Mice hung happily from her arms.

"I thought we could do an introduction, since little Miss Hermeowone is feeling bolder," George explained.

She didn't need to elaborate on why she'd chosen Anne Mice, however. The gray tabby got along with absolutely everyone—people and cats alike. If Hermeowone was going to take to any of the cats downstairs, it would be Annie.

But as George walked closer, a low growl reverberated through the gray-and-white cat at Lou's feet. Hermeowone slowly arched her back, punctuating everything with a hiss.

"Okaaay, so maybe she's not cool with other cats." George wrinkled her nose.

"What about Sapphy?" Lou asked, knowing her deaf, white cat had a calmness about him that settled other cats.

George retreated into the bookshop, returning with Sapphire. But Hermeowone's reaction was the same.

"Maybe she needs to be somewhere that she can be an only cat." Lou worried her lip between her teeth, knowing that place wouldn't be here.

Before they could discuss it further, Lou received a text from Ruby.

"It's time." Lou's eyes flashed up to meet George's.

Excitement tightened her posture. "Okay. I'll leave now. Come on, Sapph. I'll drop you off downstairs on my way."

"I'm here if you need anything," Lou called after her.

As George's footsteps echoed down the staircase, Lou moved from the couch to the chair by the window, turning off the lamps all except the small light attached to her book so she could see out onto the street. George's car turned down Thread Lane and followed a dark BMW. It was hard not to continue looking up from her book now that she was seated by the window. People walking by, bundled up in thick jackets, rushed from one destination to the next in the misty rain. In the mixture of darkness and streetlights, everything seemed to glow in the haze of moisture sitting heavy over Button.

As Lou alternated between staring out the window and reading, a cat jumped into her lap. Living with so many cats, such a thing was a daily occurrence, and Lou thought nothing of it, initially.

But then she remembered that all the cats were downstairs right now. All except the little scaredy-cat, Hermeowone. Lou held perfectly still as the previously scared cat settled onto her lap. She wasn't purring, but she seemed more relaxed than she had been since Robin dropped her off.

Not wanting to jinx the situation, Lou continued to read, only glancing up to check out the window if she saw movement.

About ten minutes after George left, Lou saw a car slow before moving toward the roundabout in the center of downtown. The back left light had a hole in it, white light streaming through, so much brighter than the light filtered through the red plastic of the brake lights.

Lou took a gulp of air. The car Willow had seen drop off the book with the note from the killer yesterday?

Instead of going through the roundabout, however, the car pulled over, parking in front of the ice cream shop next door. This was her chance. She could see who it was.

She tensed, readying herself to stand, but then she

remembered Hermeowone in her lap. And her cold. Just as with the Diana task, it seemed she would need to delegate this one as well.

She texted Easton.

> Car matching Willow's description of the one that dropped that book off at the Little Free Library is parked in front of Candy Buttons right now. It might not be for long, though.

Easton sent back a thumbs-up, and Lou put her book down so she could watch the street like it was a thrilling television show.

She could barely see through the rain gathering in droplets on her window. Then the driver must've climbed back into the car, because the brake lights turned on once more.

Oh no. They're leaving. Lou tapped her fingers on her phone, wondering if she should call Easton to let him know he should hurry. She refrained, knowing he was probably getting there as fast as he could, and her interrupting him would only slow him down.

The car pulled away.

Hope leaked out of her, making her wish she'd just scooped the cat off her lap and gone after them herself. Just as Lou was about to text Easton that they were gone, red and blue flashing lights strobed through the dark downtown section of Thread Lane as Easton pulled in behind the car. Using their indicator, the mystery car took a right, presumably to find a place to pull over.

Lou let herself exhale a quiet celebration, then went back to her book. But she couldn't read more than a paragraph before checking her phone again. Whether for an update from Easton or George, she didn't care. She just wanted to know what was going on.

About forty-five minutes later, she got her wish, all at once. Multiple sets of shoes clomped up the staircase into her apartment.

The sound scared Hermeowone off Lou's lap, and she stood to face whatever was approaching. First, George stomped in, her expression hard, her shoulders set. She was quickly followed by Wesley Saint James, who immediately helped himself to an apple on her counter. Finally, Easton walked into the apartment, wearing an air of wariness as plain as the badge he wore on a chain around his neck.

Lou didn't know who to talk to first. George's obvious anger was the one thing that tipped the scales in her direction.

"How'd the stakeout go?" Lou asked, adopting Easton's same wary posture. "Did you see who Diana met with?"

Easton stepped forward. "Wait. Stakeout?" Any apprehension he'd previously felt was replaced with alarm. He turned to George. "Why were you staking out one of my suspects?"

"Oh, it was just for Ruby, to see who Diana was considering selling the Bean and Button to," Lou explained, conveniently leaving out the part about how they, too, wondered if she might've been the one to kill her husband.

"Yeah." Wesley stepped forward. "Don't worry, Detective. She had me there the whole time to protect her."

George's poor attitude suddenly made more sense.

"Wesley, how'd you worm your way into going on the stakeout with George?" Lou blinked in confusion.

"I have my ways." He winked at her.

The cool glare she gave him following that wink caused his attention to shift to the apple in his hand, and he took another bite.

"Yeah, the same ways that he found out you and Noah are in a relationship, and that everyone knows but me." George's words were sharp as they cut through the air, directed at Lou.

Breath shoved its way out of Lou's lungs, as if George's words had actually struck her.

"I wouldn't say *everyone*. It's just me and Willow," Easton said, but he studied his shoes when George leveled him with a glare.

"You don't trust me?" The hurt in her tone stabbed at Lou's heart.

"George, it's not that. We were keeping it from everyone until we could tell Marigold. Easton and Willow? Well, I told them before I knew Noah wanted to keep it just between us." Lou narrowed her eyes, glancing from Easton to George.

Easton's shoulders were hunched as if he wished he could back out of the room to avoid the conflict.

"How'd you find out?" Lou asked.

George jabbed a thumb over her shoulder toward Wes. "This one climbed in the car with me on my way out to follow Diana. He let it slip about halfway through."

Wesley flinched. "Sorry. I thought she knew."

"I'm going to bed." George stomped past them.

"What about Diana? Did you see who she was meeting with?" Easton was interested now that he'd heard.

"It was Cassidy. Sales meeting must've meant selling her house, not her business. Don't worry, I already texted Ruby," George muttered, then closed her door.

Diana is selling the house? Lou tried to work through the recalibration she had to do with that new information, but her brain was still foggy from the cold.

Wesley backed away slowly. "Well, I think that's my cue. Lady. Gent." He bowed and headed downstairs.

Lou motioned to the table. "Did you catch the person in the car?" she asked as they both sat.

Easton sighed, showing her not to get her hopes up. "It was a teenager. He said he was picking up a delivery at the grocery store, and 'some lady' approached him with the book." Easton used finger quotes and flattened his tone to show his distaste. "She told him to drop it off at the Little Free Library and gave him a twenty to do so. He couldn't even tell me her hair color. Said he thought it was brown but couldn't be sure."

There was something about getting older that made a woman feel invisible. This was confirmation that it was true.

"Okay. Thanks. Sorry it wasn't a better lead." Lou was tired again, and her sinus headache was back. All she wanted was to take some cold medicine and go to sleep.

Easton left, and Lou went to bed. But she set an alarm, knowing she might not be able to count on George to run the bookshop for her again tomorrow.

In the minutes it took for the cold medicine to work, Lou thought through a plan to apologize to George for keeping her out of the loop. Even in her worst-case wonderings, she hadn't foreseen George getting so upset that they'd kept their relationship a secret.

CHAPTER 19

L ou woke, bleary-eyed, to her alarm the next morning. A text from Noah sat on her phone as well.

Any word from George about who Diana
met with?

She must've passed out before he'd sent that last night. Squinting at the clock, she responded.

It was Cassidy. Apparently, Diana wants to
sell her house, not the business.

Noah was up already, because he sent a message back immediately.

Huh. Seeing Cass today when she drops
off Marigold. Will see what I can find out.

Lou sent a thumbs-up and peeled herself out of bed. She

breathed through the aching pain from the remnants of a sinus headache and prepped to talk to George.

But Lou didn't even get the chance to talk to her. The apartment was empty, save for Lou and Hermeowone. George had left a note on the kitchen counter.

I'll be out all day for appointments. Will feed the cats downstairs and put Geralt in the office so he doesn't cause anyone to sprain an ankle while I'm gone.

Lou studied Hermeowone, and she swore the cat looked just as disappointed as she felt.

She felt slightly better after a shower and a cup of coffee, but she kept her slippers on as she padded down the stairs into the bookshop, reveling in the small bit of comfort while she did her opening chores. Lou reluctantly switched out her slippers for shoes only minutes before she unlocked the front door and turned the sign.

There must've been a fair bit of wind overnight because the oak trees from Willow had lost more leaves, the evidence of which was scattered over the sidewalk in front of the bookstore. The sun was shining, and it wasn't raining, though. Lou cracked the door to check the temperature and found that even though it was sunny outside, it was still chilly. Shivering, she pulled the door shut and started a fire.

Silas and Cricket bustled inside a few minutes later.

"Oh, that feels wonderful." Cricket sidled up to the cast-iron stove and rubbed her hands together.

Silas shuffled over to the seating area, pulling a newspaper from where he'd tucked it under his arm. The moment he sat down, the sound of his newspaper unfolding, snapping through the space, Catnip Everdeen slunk out from wherever she'd been hiding and jumped up to sit next to him. A small grin twitched at the corners of the older man's mouth.

"You look like you feel awful, my dear." Cricket leaned on the checkout counter and peered at Lou.

Taking a step back, Lou said, "Well, then I look how I feel." She winced.

"Where's George?" Silas craned his neck as he searched for the young woman.

Lou swallowed, buying herself time to work through the complicated emotions surrounding George at the moment. "She had appointments," was all she said.

"I would volunteer to watch the place, but I have another embroidery class today, and I have to get my samples ready," Cricket said.

"That's okay." Lou smiled at her. "I'm feeling a little better now that I'm down here. Maybe getting back to my routine will help me heal."

Cricket snapped her fingers. "Oh, I was going to mention…"

Given Lou's history with the woman, she expected something about Godfrey's case to come out of Cricket's mouth next. She'd been the one who'd been so interested in looking into the BBS after all. To be fair, it seemed that her prediction about Godfrey's death being an inside job had been correct, now that they'd learned of Sasha's return to Godfrey's back porch after the meeting.

But Cricket surprised Lou when, instead, she said, "One of my students in class was talking about how she's looking for a cat, especially one who might not be desirable to others. I mentioned Whiskers and Words, but she's worried about adopting a cat without knowing how it'll do in her home." The woman's eyes narrowed. "Do you ever do trial periods for the adoptions?"

Lou bobbed her head, catching up with the new topic. "Absolutely." The goal wasn't merely to find each cat *a* home, but the *right* home. "Who is it?"

"Harmony Lofall," Cricket said.

Lou's expression softened. "I met her and her sister … well, when Godfrey…" She didn't need to finish that sentence.

Cricket clicked her tongue. "Harmony is trying to get out a little more, so she's been taking my classes, and I think she and her sister get a little lonely with just the two of them in that house."

"Do you know what kind of cat she's hoping for?"

In Lou's peripheral vision, Silas placed a protective hand on Catnip, as if to will them not to want her. Lou would be silly to adopt out Catnip Everdeen, especially since Silas was the only person the cat truly liked.

Cricket raked her teeth across her bottom lip. "Well, she said she stopped in the other day to meet the cats, and she found one who really seemed to like her."

Lou hadn't seen Harmony come into the shop.

"She said you weren't here. It was George behind the counter," Cricket said, waving a hand toward Lou. "The cat that she really connected with was Meatball, but she wasn't sure if she was up for adoption since you haven't made her a profile sheet yet."

Lou zeroed in on the small tortoiseshell lounging by the fire. She hadn't been in a rush to find a home for Meatball, but she knew if she ever did, it would have to be a home without men, given her unknown, but obviously traumatic, past with them. It was why she'd held off on making up an adoption sheet like she'd done with the others. But, as Lou considered the Lofall sisters, she realized it might be a great fit, especially if Meatball had connected with Harmony in the shop.

"Meatball might be perfect for them. I can definitely bring her over after the shop closes today, if that works for Harmony." Lou's heart tugged at the thought of losing the sweet cat, but an environment where she wouldn't have to be around as many men might be even better for her.

"I'll let her know that." Cricket beamed.

Through the fog of her sickness, Lou remembered a question she'd wanted to ask Cricket about the case. "Cricket, has Diana Crane taken your embroidery class before?"

The woman blinked. "Diana? No. That woman doesn't do crafts."

"Then where did Godfrey get the handkerchief?" Lou had assumed he'd had it because Diana had made it for him, but if she wasn't into sewing, or any other crafts, it couldn't have been from her. But when Mitchell had told the story about him using it to clean up the mess, it had sounded like the handkerchief had been Godfrey's. "Do you remember anyone who made a handkerchief with a rose in one corner and a hummingbird in another?" Lou asked.

Cricket squinted as she thought. "Not off the top of my head, but I take pictures of the projects completed in my class. I can search through my photos."

"That would be helpful. Thanks, Cricket."

She held up a hand in a wave. "Okay, well, I'm off. I'll send you Harmony's information so you can coordinate the meet and greet."

Lou and Silas called out goodbyes to Cricket. Once she was gone, Lou put on some quiet piano music and started on some ordering in between customers. Silas headed out midmorning, but she almost didn't notice, given how busy it was. Other than being a Friday—one of her better sales days, historically—the morning sun was soon hidden behind a bank of gray clouds, and Lou felt the cozy book-store must've looked like a beacon to anyone wandering past on the street.

Even better, after a handful of cups of tea throughout the day, and another round of cold medicine, Lou was feeling much better. She was glad, too, because she'd been messaging with Harmony Lofall, who was incredibly excited about Meatball and wanted Lou to bring her over as soon as possible.

After closing the shop that day, Lou loaded Meatball into one of the crates and drove over to Harmony Lofall's home. She couldn't help focusing on Diana Crane's home as she drove to the next house over. Had she and Godfrey been planning on selling the house before he'd been killed, or was she trying to get away from the memory of him, or her possible guilt, Lou wondered.

Harmony met Lou at the door, excitement leaking from her tight posture. "Come in." She beckoned her forward.

Lou barely got into the sitting room at the front of the house before Harmony was next to her, wiggling her fingers in anticipation of Lou opening the crate and letting out the cat.

Patting the air with her hands to calm the woman, Lou said, "Meatball is very sweet, but if she feels overwhelmed, she'll do a crouching walk and will want to hide." Lou had seen some of that behavior at Sebastian's, when he'd been explaining the cat's fear of men.

Harmony straightened. Now that the woman was fairly still, Lou bent and unlatched the metal door of the crate, letting it swing open. She stepped back a few feet, giving the cat space and time to come out on her own terms.

Meatball's pink nose stuck out first, wiggling in the air as she sniffed the new space. Her golden yellow eyes were enormous and round as she stared up at Lou. They seemed to hold a million questions about why she was there and when they would get to leave. Harmony gasped and covered her mouth with her hands. The woman was practically buzzing.

But that seemed to be the very last kind of energy Meatball wanted to be around because she slunk out of the crate and crouched down, so her belly practically touched the floor. She skittered and hid between the legs of a chair under the dining room table.

It was interesting, since Lou hadn't seen her act like that when she'd first come to the bookshop.

"Let's allow her time and space to explore," Lou said, all too aware of the defeat already weighing down Harmony's previously excited posture.

The cat darted behind a couch it seemed like no one ever sat on, and then moved into the next room. Harmony and Lou followed a few seconds later to give her space. Meatball let out a few low meows, and she scanned the room, as if searching for her feline friends.

Lou couldn't help but notice how tense the woman was. She wondered if Meatball could be feeding off that energy, and that was what was making her so nervous.

"How'd your show turn out?" Lou asked in an attempt to get the woman to loosen up. When Harmony shot her a confused scowl, Lou added, "The one you and Mariah were watching the other day. Was it about getting married to strangers?"

Harmony's face relaxed. "Oh! Yes, that one. We're still in the middle of it. Each episode is so long, and sometimes we get behind because we agreed not to watch them without one another."

"What's going on this season?" Lou asked.

A smile took over Harmony's expression as she launched into a detailed explanation of the different couples who she hoped would stay together, and those she didn't think would make it. The woman's shoulders relaxed, and they followed the cat into the living room.

Unlike the other room, which looked like it was rarely used, this room had a cozy couch with blankets draped across the back. A coffee table held a stack of books, a clear sign of a to-be-read pile. The book on top held a bookmark toward the end, showing Lou whoever was reading it was almost finished.

She studied the rest of the room. There wasn't a television anywhere. The sisters had been so animated when talking about the reality television show they loved, and how many times they'd watched it, that Lou had expected a TV to be a big part of their décor. But as she stood there in the last room—she could see beyond the bedrooms and bathroom down the hall—and she'd yet to see a sign of one. Thinking back to the first room they were in, Lou wondered if one of the pieces of art on the wall could've been one of those fancy televisions that disguises itself as a painting when it's not in use.

But before Lou could ask about it, Harmony knelt down and reached out to pet Meatball. The cat's ears flattened, and she reached forward with her paw, scratching Harmony's hand in warning.

"Ouch!" Harmony reared back, clutching her hand. She turned to Lou, sadness written all over her face. "I don't think she likes it here."

"I hate to agree," Lou said. "But she doesn't seem comfortable. I think it might have more to do with her wanting to be around the other cats at the shop than her disliking your home. Still, maybe Meatball isn't the cat for you."

Harmony's shoulders slumped forward. "Which means

none of your cats are because I didn't bond with any of them more than her at the shop the other day."

"Not *all* of them," Lou said slowly, thinking of Hermeowone. And even though the little cat was only just warming up to her, Lou had a feeling that she couldn't discount the match. The fact that Harmony liked to read—the thing that had helped Hermeowone open up to Lou—made Lou wonder if the cat would make an exception to live in this quieter house.

Whereas Meatball seemed to miss the other cats, Hermeowone had all but freaked out whenever they'd even let her see another cat. A one-cat house like this one might be just what she needed.

"We can try with her tomorrow if that works for you," Lou suggested.

Harmony's shoulders pulled up in anticipation. "That's great. I can't wait."

Lou couldn't either, and for the sake of the woman, hoped this match stuck.

CHAPTER 20

Lou and Meatball returned to the bookshop. The other cats crowded around the tortoiseshell, thoroughly interested in the smell of the Lofall sisters' house on her fur, but eventually rubbed up against her in acceptance. Any happiness at the sight of the cat going back to her normal self was stolen away when she noticed the office door open at the back of the bookshop.

George had taken Geralt. A note was stuck to the office door.

Geralt and I are at Brynn's.

Lou's heart ached, and she wondered briefly if she should drive out to Pine Farm and talk to George. But she wasn't sure that would help. It was possible that George just needed her space. The other obstacle standing in the way of that plan was the rescheduled town council meeting happening in less than an hour.

Between George being out of town, and the text she'd gotten from Noah while she was at the Lofalls' home saying that he was going to skip the meeting to have a celebratory dinner out with Marigold—she'd finally turned in the dreaded science fair project—Lou knew Cricket and the opposing side would need all the help they could get with the vote.

So she got the cats fed and left for the community center. It was packed, and a wobbly feeling teetered in Lou's gut as she wondered if the BBS had really convinced the people they needed to represent their side of the issue at hand.

It wasn't as if Lou had truly intended on trying to find more votes for the BBS, nor had she promised to do so, but guilt about deceiving them still clung to her like droplets of rain as she entered the community center.

Mitchell paced near the back of the space. Lou sidled up to him.

"Ready?" she asked.

He lifted his brows in lieu of an answer.

"Nervous?" She eyed his hands, twitching now that he'd forced his feet to stay in one spot.

He gave Lou a wan smile. "A little. I know we can always bring the vote again if it doesn't pass tonight. But the next voting cycle feels a long way off."

"True." Lou worked up as much sympathy as she could muster.

As they stood there, locals filed into the gym and found their seats, and a question that had been bugging Lou surfaced. She turned toward Mitchell.

"Hey, remember when you were telling me about the

handkerchief that Godfrey used to clean up his spill during the last BBS meeting at his house?"

Mitchell blew air through distended nostrils by way of an affirmative answer.

"Do you remember where he got it?" Lou asked, appraising the man. "Like, was it on the counter, or did someone hand it to him?"

His forehead had scrunched together as Lou had been asking her questions, but as she finished, his brows shot up, and recognition sparkled behind his brown eyes. "It was Sasha. She handed it over. But I don't remember her taking it with her."

Lou gulped. *Because she left it there*, she thought to herself, saying aloud a quick, "Thank you. I'd better find my seat." Her gaze flicked around the room, searching for Easton. He needed to know this as soon as possible.

Mitchell stopped her, placing a hand on her arm. "I just wanted to say a quick thank you."

Guilt wrapped around Lou's lungs, making it hard to breathe. But Mitchell didn't thank her for her help with the BBS.

"I got the call from Sebastian today, offering me the job of editor-in-chief of the *Button Post*." Mitchell straightened his spine with pride, standing even taller than he had before.

Lou beamed. "Congratulations. That's great news. But, what does that have to do with me?"

Mitchell appraised her. "Sebastian said that someone he trusted very much had given him the impression that I would be great for the job. I know you're close with him, and I appreciate the good word." The older man winked.

Lou bit down on her lip to hold in the smile that threatened at the corners of her mouth. Little did Mitchell know, but the person Sebastian had been referring to was likely Wesley. Lou didn't want to call attention to how Sebastian had ordered his PI to follow the candidates, though, so she simply said, "I'm very glad you got the job. I know you'll be great."

Waving to Mitchell, Lou wandered over toward the rows of chairs set up for the meeting. Cricket lifted her chin in greeting as Lou approached, having saved a few seats in the middle of the space. The woman grunted a response but seemed preoccupied as she sat rigid in her chair.

Unlike the last meeting, where the sides were divided, it seemed as if they were all muddled together this time. But Lou didn't miss that the other three members of the BBS scowled in her direction as they noticed who she sat next to.

Luckily, Willow arrived a few seconds later, giving Lou a reason to glance away from the BBS members and taking up the final seat Cricket had saved.

"Is Easton coming?" Lou whispered.

Willow gave a quick jerk of her head. "Stuck at the station."

Cricket huffed, mumbling something about everyone on her side bailing, and Lou let some of her worries move to the upcoming vote. Cricket was right. There were quite a few less people present than there had been at the last meeting. Would that work to their advantage or against?

"Sasha Richards never took your embroidery class, did

she?" Lou asked, leaning closer to Cricket so she could keep her voice down.

"Nope," Cricket answered quickly, not even needing to think about it. "And I checked my photos for that handkerchief you mentioned. Wherever it came from, it wasn't from one of my classes."

Lou contemplated that, nodding in thanks to Cricket for searching.

Kyle Goldblume banged the gavel he held, from his seat at the center of the long table. "Okay, everyone. We only have one item on the agenda today since this is a special meeting. We'll be moving right on to the vote."

From the front row, Robin raised her hand and said, "Mr. Chairman, don't forget the special request."

Kyle cleared his throat. "Right. For this vote, the Button Beautification Society would like to make a slight change and turn it into an anonymous vote. It will take a little longer to count the votes, but we'll get everyone out of here as soon as we can, and we thank you in advance for your patience."

Mitchell finally threaded his way through the chairs and sat next to the rest of the BBS. When he turned his attention toward Lou, however, there wasn't judgment behind his gaze, as there had been with his fellow committee members. In fact, it seemed like Lou's question about the handkerchief had caused a riptide of thoughts to grab at the older man's mind, and he glared at Sasha, seated two chairs down from him.

"Please make sure you clearly mark the for-or-against box of your choice with a dark X or a clear check mark,"

Kyle explained from the front of the room, pulling Lou back to the vote.

Another council member walked along the rows of chairs, stopping to distribute stacks of half sheets of paper with the proposal typed out and a space for each person present to vote underneath. Lou quickly marked the *against* box before folding the thing in half. She was thankful they'd gone for the anonymous vote. Based on the way the BBS members were already glaring at her for her choice of seat, it would've looked even worse had she been forced to hold her hand up for the against vote. Passing the ballots forward, the same council member collected them, bringing them up to the table at the front of the room.

Tension spread through the gymnasium as delicate as the thin spiderwebs decorating their town as they sank deeper into fall. The council members whispered, having turned off their microphones as they counted the ballots.

Minutes that felt like hours later, Kyle stood, holding up the microphone. "In the proposition to move the Button Beautification Society's town-theme proposal forward to a ballot measure, those for were forty-six."

Lou's pulse increased as her gaze flitted about the room, wondering what percentage of the people present that number represented.

But she didn't need to worry, because Kevin quickly added, "And those against were seventy-two. Which means the measure will not move forward on the next ballot."

The end of Kyle's statement was drowned out by cheers. Cricket finally cracked a smile.

"They're not the only ones who were busy this week," the woman said.

Ah, Lou realized. *That's why Cricket hasn't been helping with the case. She's been working on making sure the vote didn't pass.*

Lou chuckled. "Then why did you seem so worried when I sat down?"

"I didn't want to jinx myself," she scoffed. "I didn't know how much the BBS had done or how many people they'd recruited over the week."

But any feelings of celebration were cut short as a screech erupted from their left. Everyone quieted, many sitting back in their seats, so it was easy to spot where the cry had originated.

Sasha Richards was standing in the middle of the space, her fingers curled like claws and her breaths ragged. "So it was all for nothing?" she yelled the question as her fingers tugged at her hair. "Everything we worked for, thrown out because of Crane?" And even though she'd specifically mentioned Crane, her ire landed on Lou. "You!" She jabbed a finger forward and struggled through the crowd. "It's all your fault. You sabotaged everything."

Lou pushed back her shoulders, not about to let this woman bully her. Cricket straightened where she sat next to her.

"I'm sorry you lost, Sasha. Maybe it was more about the town not wanting to be told what to do instead of a personal vendetta against you. Did you ever think about that?" Lou kept her voice level.

Sasha let out a feral scream. Based on the disheveled

state of her hair and clothes, added to the dark circles around her eyes, Lou would've bet anything that she hadn't been getting enough sleep over the past week. The woman wasn't in her right mind.

"You'll pay for this," Sasha said as Adam dragged her back, whispering warnings in her ear. "I'll make sure you regret messing with us."

A shiver wound through Lou. Cricket placed a supportive hand on her arm. Willow, taller than the average woman, straightened and stood in front of Lou.

"Would you like to make those threats with a member of the Button Police Department nearby?" she asked coolly.

Adam's jaw ticked and his nostrils flared, but he guided the struggling Sasha away and down the hallway.

Willow turned to Lou, the worry she'd been keeping under wraps finally showing in her expression as her blue eyes met Lou's.

"We need to call Easton. Now." Lou's voice was strangled.

"I don't think they'd actually do anything to you," Willow said. "That was just a reaction to the vote."

Lou wished that was all, but she said, "No, we need to tell Easton that the handkerchief that was covering Godfrey's face belonged to Sasha, and that after that outburst, I'm even more convinced she was the one who pulled the trigger and killed him."

CHAPTER 21

Easton paced through his office, digesting the information Lou and Willow had just shared. "Even though Diana's out, I'm still not sure this will be enough to bring in Sasha."

"Diana's out?" Willow asked.

Easton wet his lips. "She met with Cass the night George followed her, but it turned out she'd already met with the corporate person Godfrey had been talking to. It was why she flew home early and didn't tell anyone but a few close friends. The offer, however, turned out to be so bad, that she called him to yell at him for even considering it."

"The call the BBS overheard," Lou said with a crisply indrawn breath.

Easton started pacing again when Lou received a text from Noah.

Hope the meeting went well. Want to join
us for dinner at the pizza place?

Lou wanted nothing more than to meet up with them at the pizza parlor after the meeting. But she knew the plan was to tell Marigold tomorrow, and she didn't know how well she could hold anything back after being sick and then enduring that awful meeting. Plus, the pizza parlor wasn't exactly a safe space for her, not since Sasha had threatened her at the meeting.

She also didn't know how much longer Easton would need to talk to her. Given how tired and sick she felt, she hoped it wouldn't be too long.

> Meeting went okay. Vote didn't pass. I'm still not feeling great, so I think I'm going to head home.

Noah responded with a thumbs-up, letting Lou return her waning attention to the detective.

"But Peanut Butter didn't react to Sasha, did he?" Easton asked. At first, Lou thought he was talking to her, but a voice came from behind her.

"Not any of the times I was with him." Brenner stood in the doorway when Lou glanced over her shoulder, obviously back from the wedding.

Willow eyed Lou, wincing as she took in her friend's slowly sinking posture. "Well, you two can figure that out on your own. I think Lou needs to get home. Want me to come with you, just in case?" Willow scowled in Lou's direction, but she knew it wasn't directed at her as much as it was at the memory of Sasha's threats.

Easton adopted a similar expression. "We can send an officer detail to the bookshop if you'd like."

"I'm okay." Lou held up a hand as if that might stop the worrying. "I'm sure it was an empty threat. I mostly just need to get some sleep." She turned to Willow. "I'll let you know if I need anything, but as for now, I just want to have a quiet night at home with the cats."

Leaving before her best friend could dote on her more, Lou stopped at the grocery store to grab some ingredients since she finally felt well enough to eat something other than soup.

She was looking forward to finishing the book she'd been reading, but when she drove up Thimble Drive on her way home after the store, she quickly realized relaxing wasn't going to be in the cards for her tonight.

The right front window of the bookshop was broken, the gaping hole in the middle made the remaining shards of glass that hung there look like jagged teeth in a sinister smile.

The cats.

Lou screeched to a halt in the parking spot in front of the shop, not even bothering to park around the back. Once out of her car, she opened the front door with shaking fingers that jingled her keys unhelpfully, taking her longer than usual to unlock the door.

A large rock sat among the shards of broken glass on the floor, right next to the register. But as she checked around, she couldn't see any signs of the cats. Sure, the hole was farther up the window, but they could've jumped out.

Moving toward the back of the shop, Lou couldn't seem to force any words from her tight throat, so she raced through the bookstore in silence as she searched for the cats.

Finally, a flash of white fur caught her eye in the used book section. Sapphire's bright blue eyes blinked back at her from under one of the taller bookshelves. To his right, tucked in the small space, was Anne Mice. Charles Lickens and Catnip Everdeen weren't too far off to the right. Finally, Lou spotted Meatball, her darker fur making her blend in better in the shadows. Lou pulled out her phone.

Fingers shaking, she called Easton.

"Change your mind about the patrol already?" he asked, the lightness in his tone feeling wholly unnatural, given the state of her shop. "Willow just left. Is she not answering her phone again?"

"Easton, someone broke the front window of the bookstore." Her voice shook, mirroring the rest of her.

"What?" There was a pause as he seemed to sit in disbelief for a moment. "I'm on my way."

She hung up before he could say anything else. It felt like the world around her was moving in slow motion, yet she still couldn't process everything happening.

Texting Noah, she let him know what had happened and that she and the cats were okay. He messaged back immediately.

Goldie and I are on our way.

Before she could even message Willow, a text came in from her best friend, letting her know she was en route as well.

Lou hugged her arms around herself as a brisk breeze whipped in through the gaping hole at the front of the shop. Knowing Hermeowone probably wouldn't take well to having the other cats upstairs with her, she took a moment to sequester the newest cat into the spare bedroom, open now that George wasn't staying there.

Once that was done, she let the rest of the small herd of cats up into the apartment. Because they'd been kept out of it for the better part of a week, the group raced upstairs. Lou was just coming back down when cars began pulling up in front of the store.

First, there was Easton, followed a few seconds later by Noah and Marigold. Willow wasn't far behind. They all took their turns gaping at the hole and pulling Lou into hugs, glad to hear the cats were all unharmed. Marigold went upstairs to be with the cats while the adults surveyed the damage downstairs.

"That's it," Easton said. "This has to be enough to arrest Sasha. If you all have this under control, I'm going to see if I can't get a warrant to bring her in."

Willow, Noah, and Lou nodded, and Easton took off.

"What was Sasha thinking?" Willow grabbed the brooms and dustpans from the back office.

"She could've easily hurt one of the cats," Noah said.

Lou agreed. Anger boiled under the surface of her skin, and she was just about to let it out when another car pulled up in front of the bookshop.

"George?" Lou exhaled the name as the young woman ran from her car and enveloped Lou in a hug.

"I'm so sorry I left," George said, the words muffled in Lou's shoulder.

Lou wrapped her arms around her tighter. "I'm glad you did. If you and Geralt were here, that would've just added more to the list of who Sasha could've hurt." She pulled back, not wanting George to catch her cold. "Did you leave Geralt with Brynn?"

George cast a glance over at her car. Two little paws perched on the window as he peered out with interest. "He wasn't too crazy about how fast I drove on the way here."

"Hey, George," Noah said as he walked by. "Good to see you. I'm going to run home and grab a sheet of plywood from my garage so we can get this covered up for tonight. It won't look amazing, but it'll keep out the cold."

Lou smiled at him in thanks. By the time he walked off, and she'd turned back to George, the young woman's face was tight with pain.

"I'm sorry we didn't tell you," Lou whispered, knowing Marigold was just upstairs.

George discharged a grunted breath. "You don't need to apologize. Honestly, I overreacted. The way I took that news had a lot more to do with some things I've been going through lately than anything to do with the two of you."

Lou grabbed her hand. "I'm always here ... whenever you're ready to talk about it."

George nodded in thanks. "Things have been confusing lately ... with Wesley."

Cocking an eyebrow, Lou gave the young woman space to add to her explanation.

She groaned. "I hate him one minute, but then the next, I

feel like I want to grab his stupid face and pull him into a kiss."

Lou's lips parted in surprise. So, Noah had been right to wonder if there wasn't something more between them after all.

"I think it's part of why I freaked out about you and Noah," George explained. "It made me realize that I wasn't being honest with myself about my feelings." Her gaze moved to the broken window. "Anyway, you have more important things on your mind right now, and I still have to figure out how I'm feeling, but once I'm ready to talk more, I'll let you know."

Lou pulled her into one last hug, and they stepped apart, turning their attention back to the cleanup. By the time Noah returned with the wood, they had all the glass taken care of.

Willow huffed out a sigh of relief as she checked her phone a few minutes later, letting everyone know Sasha was in custody, and that Easton was holding Adam for questioning as long as he could.

"You're safe tonight," Willow said to Lou with a wink.

The group left a short while later, once the window was covered and the cats were settled. George went back to Brynn's since Hermeowone was taking over the spare bedroom. Between things mending with Lou and George, and the finality of Sasha being arrested, Lou slept like a rock—even the kind that had come crashing through her window.

CHAPTER 22

Lou decided to keep the bookshop closed the following day. Even though it was a Saturday, they'd found more small shards of glass in the light of day and the plywood made the bookshop feel dark and sad, such a change from its normal warm atmosphere. Plus, she was supposed to go to Noah's that evening for dinner so they could talk to Marigold, and she wanted to keep her energy up so she could be feeling better for that meeting.

It turned out to be a good thing she didn't have to stay with the shop, because around noon, Lou got a call on the shop phone.

"Hello," she said. "This is Whiskers and Words."

"Oh good. I didn't know if you were still planning on coming today." The woman on the other end sounded anxious and familiar, but Lou couldn't place her right away.

"I'm sorry. Who is this?"

"Harmony Lofall," the woman answered. "Weren't you going to come over with the other cat today?"

It had totally slipped Lou's mind. "I'm so sorry. I forgot. We had an accident here last night and I've closed for the day." She looked upstairs, thinking about Hermeowone locked away in that guest bedroom. "But since I'm closed, it shouldn't be a big deal to come over with the cat. Is this a good time?"

"Yes, this would be perfect. I hope everything is okay, though." Concern edged the woman's voice.

"Everything's fine. We just had a scare with a window breaking," Lou said, not sure she was ready to give Sasha power over her by admitting how much the vandalism had rattled her.

Plus, what a better way to change her outlook on the day than to find a cat a new home?

They hung up, and Lou got a cat carrier ready. She loved that Hermeowone had gotten so comfortable with her that she was fine with Lou picking her up and putting her into the crate. She hoped the cat would take to Harmony and Mariah in the same way, but Lou wasn't about to push her. If she didn't seem comfortable at the Lofall house, Harmony could wait until she got a cat in that was truly right for her.

Harmony answered the door a few minutes later, and Lou stepped inside when the woman waved her forward.

"Thank you so much for coming," Harmony said. "My sister's at the store, and I'm not sure how she's going to feel about this, so I want the cat to be a sure thing before she gets home."

Lou frowned at her. "Your sister doesn't want a pet?" Lou didn't want any cat, especially one who'd had a rough start, to go into any home where they were not 100 percent wanted.

"Oh, she'll love it once it's a done deal." Harmony swatted a hand toward Lou. "It's just, well, she worries about money, and she's always talking about how we can't afford this and we can't afford that." Harmony rolled her eyes. "But a cat is such a small expense, and Mariah's been wanting me to have a friend for a while now."

Lou processed that, but instead of stopping the meet and greet, she decided to see how the cat did before making any decisions. It was likely she wouldn't be comfortable here and the point would be moot. If the cat took to Harmony, Lou would dig a little further into what she'd said about her sister.

"This is Hermeowone Granger." Lou set down the crate in the fancy front room, just as she'd done with Meatball.

The woman beamed. "Harmony and Hermeowone. We almost match."

"She was a surrender because her previous owner thought she was mean." Lou shot Harmony a look that made it clear the owner had been wrong. "She's actually very sweet, just terrified of most people."

Harmony covered her mouth with her hands as she stared at the poor creature. "That's awful. Well, I'm very passionate about giving cats a chance when other people have given up on them."

Lou carefully opened the crate door, stepping back to give Hermeowone space. Harmony followed. The cat slunk out, reminding Lou so much of how Meatball had exited the crate yesterday that Lou tensed, ready for this cat to respond to the house in the same way.

But once she caught sight of Lou, Hermeowone straightened and rushed over, winding her body around Lou's legs. The motion tugged at Lou's heart and made her wonder if she should let the cat go when she was clearly so comfortable around her. For a cat who didn't seem to trust anyone, pulling her away from the first person she'd trusted in a while didn't seem fair.

Just as Lou was about to voice her concerns, Hermeowone glanced up at Harmony, studying the woman with her big golden eyes for a few seconds. Harmony stayed put, not reaching toward her or making any move other than to let a small smile pull at her lips as she blinked slowly back at the cat. Then she looked away, giving the cat a break from the small amount of eye contact.

Hermeowone strutted forward and wound around Harmony's legs in the same way she'd done with Lou's. Harmony pressed her lips together with excitement as Lou met her wide-eyed gaze. Lou couldn't keep the grin from her face if she'd tried.

"That's amazing," she whispered. "It took me days to get that far with her."

Harmony beamed with pride. "Should we move to the couch?" she whispered, pointing to the cozier living room.

Lou led the way, and they walked carefully down the short hallway. Hermeowone followed on their heels. Harmony settled onto the couch, leaving the armchair by the stack of books open for Lou. They sat in silence as

Hermeowone sniffed a few things and then jumped up on the couch next to Harmony.

It was then that Lou noticed the sewing machine on a table in the corner of the room. Had it been there the last time she'd visited?

"That's a nice machine. Are you using that to practice the embroidery techniques you're learning with Cricket?" Lou asked.

Harmony practically guffawed, almost scaring away the cat. "No, that's my sister's machine. She won't let me touch it. Says I'll mess it up, and it's her baby."

"Does she embroider too?" Lou asked.

Harmony nodded. "I'm always telling her she could sell her stuff, but she says it's just a hobby."

"Is there a reason she doesn't teach you?" Lou asked. "Why pay to take a class from Cricket if you have an expert sewer in your home?" It seemed like the sisters did everything together, and if they were worried about money, a sewing class seemed like an unnecessary expense.

"That's true." Harmony tipped her head to one side. "She said she wanted me to get out more, but maybe it's more that she would get frustrated trying to teach me." The sister shrugged it off and refocused on the cat next to her.

"I think she really likes you." Lou felt any worry release from her bones. That time, the cat hadn't even come to her first, meaning she really was feeling good around Harmony.

Harmony gently placed her hand next to the cat on the couch, letting her smell it first before caressing it over her back. But instead of shying away, Hermeowone arched up into the touch, eliciting a squeak of excitement from Lou.

That was nothing compared to the happiness they both felt as the cat climbed into Harmony's lap.

All right. Well, that seemed to settle it. The cat was a good fit here, which meant Lou needed to dig a little more about the things Harmony had mentioned about her sister's hesitation surrounding a pet.

"So…" Lou said, careful not to stare at the cat in Harmony's lap. "You said your sister is worried about money. Are you sure she'll be okay with a cat?"

Harmony chanced a quick kiss on the top of Hermeowone's head. The cat allowed it. "I know she will be. She likes cats, but she just worries. She's my older sister and can't help it. Really, though, a cat won't cost enough to concern her."

"Are you sure?" Lou pushed. "Their day-to-day expenses might not be too steep, but what if they have to see the vet or have surgery? That can add up quickly."

"True." Harmony dipped her head, using the gesture to plant two more kisses on the cat's head. "To be honest, I think a lot of her stress about money is gone now that we don't have to worry about Godfrey anymore."

Lou's forehead wrinkled. "What do you mean?"

"He was always threatening to report us to the HOA. We're both retired, so we're on fixed incomes, and we don't have a lot of extra money for things like landscaping or yard work. Mariah used to do more of it because I have a bad back, but she's been tiring out a lot quicker lately, and it's been hard for us to mow the lawn or weed, something

Godfrey was constantly on us about. She even went to talk to him about it last week, to get him to see our side of things."

"How'd that go?" Lou cringed.

Harmony sighed. "Not great, but now … well, now we don't have to worry."

Lou normally wouldn't have thought twice about a comment surrounding money like that, but she was always more thorough when she was looking at a home for one of her foster cats. She wanted to make sure it was a safe place, the best place possible.

She remembered back to the night she and Noah found Godfrey's body. The Lofall sisters had talked about how they hadn't heard anything like a gunshot because they'd been watching their favorite reality television show. But the lack of a television made Lou's stomach churn with unease.

"I'm sorry if this is a silly question," Lou said, "but where's your TV? I didn't see one in either room we were in, and I figured you would have one with how much you talked about your marrying strangers show."

Harmony waved a hand at Lou. "Oh, we don't have one out here. Mariah and I each have one in our bedrooms."

Understanding washed over Lou. "So, whose room do you watch your show in?"

"We split up," Harmony said. "But we text throughout, so it's like we're watching in the same room, but instead we're each cozy in our own beds."

"Wait. So when you said you were watching your reality show during the window Godfrey was shot, you weren't in the same room?"

"No, but I know Mariah was next door," Harmony said defensively, as if she could tell what Lou was hinting at.

"How?"

Harmony scoffed, "We were texting, like I said."

"The whole time?" Lou fixed her with a stare.

"Well…" Harmony's eyes flicked around the room. "Mariah must've fallen asleep, because she didn't text back for a while, but she's been doing that a lot lately. I told you; she's been a lot sleepier as of late."

Lou ticked through the things that were not in Mariah's favor. She was worried about money, Godfrey was constantly threatening to report them to the Forest Pond HOA, which would've resulted in fines they couldn't afford, and if the Button Beautification Society's theme proposition had passed, that would've meant even more money to pay for the change in house color.

Harmony laughed nervously, as if she could tell what Lou was thinking. "She just worries. But I have to remind her that her favorite book to quote at me talks about living in the here and now." She snorted as she motioned to the stack of books next to the couch.

The here and now was definitely a line from the—yep, she could see a worn copy of *The Organization Man* by W. H. Whyte, just like the copy that had been placed in the Little Free Library. Well, not *just* like it. This copy was worn, as if the owner had read it over and over. Lou rationalized that someone wouldn't be silly enough to leave their personal copy of their favorite book, especially if they were trying to keep the police's eye away from them.

"Harmony," Lou said her name in a whisper. "How sure

are you that your sister was here between the hours of eleven and three on the day Godfrey was shot?"

Harmony gasped, but even that sound didn't make the skittish cat jump off her lap. "Why would you ask that?" But from the way her eyes narrowed and widened again, she could guess.

"I think your sister might have had reason to hurt Godfrey. When you said the two of you were watching your show together, Easton probably didn't think twice about you because there was an alibi. But if Mariah was in another room, and didn't respond to your texts … I think she could've been next door."

And, if she embroiders, the handkerchief could've been hers, left there when she confronted him last week, Lou thought, keeping that tidbit to herself.

Lou realized, then, that Peanut Butter hadn't stopped in front of the Crane household the other day on their walk. He'd been trying to tell them it was the Lofall house where he recognized the smell on the handkerchief.

Harmony frowned, as if it couldn't possibly be true. But then her expression relaxed, and she seemed to understand why Lou suspected her sister. It was so mesmerizing to watch the woman come to terms with the truth—that her sister might've taken her protective streak too far—that Lou didn't notice Harmony's eyes flash up to the space behind Lou until it was too late.

Before she could turn around, something hit the back of Lou's head, and darkness took over her vision.

CHAPTER 23

L ou's head pounded, and her vision was still blurred as she blinked open her eyes. Her eyes cleared the more she blinked, and she tried to move, but Lou's breath caught as she realized her arms wouldn't budge.

They were tied behind her back.

Shifting her feet, she found them equally immovable. Her surroundings came into focus as she struggled. She was in the fancy living room of the Lofall house, the one that looked like it never had anyone sitting in it. Except, ironically, there she was, tied to a chair in the middle of the space.

Mariah perched on the couch across from Lou, her head in her hands. Harmony paced in the space behind her sister, holding on to the cat, noticing first that Lou was awake. Her attention locked on to Lou, and she gave her the most apologetic of grimaces. Lou had no doubt she hadn't known what her sister would do.

But Harmony's stillness alerted Mariah because she lifted her gaze. Her eyes weren't apologetic like her sister's. No. Mariah's were cold, calculating, resigned.

"You just couldn't leave it alone, could you?" Her words sliced across the room, making Lou shiver.

She wouldn't show that fear, however. Lou narrowed her eyes and spit out, "I could say the same thing to you."

When Mariah tilted her head in question, Lou continued.

"The handkerchief? The book in the little library? The note? Was the rock through my window you too?" Each question hit Mariah, but they only made her look even more smug.

The older woman clapped her hands quietly, mockingly, in Lou's direction. "I'll admit, I was having too much fun watching the group of you flounder from one suspect to another. It wasn't as if you were getting close. Diana and Sasha just kept making it too easy." She giggled, but any humor behind the gesture was too soaked in malice that it couldn't be compared to the happy origin of the sound. "And then I saw you putting up that little library, and I just couldn't help myself."

"So the *I killed him, but not for the reason you think* was to push us toward … who?" Lou asked.

Mariah jerked her shoulders up. "I didn't overthink it. It was true, so I wrote it."

"What was the reason behind killing Godfrey, then?" Lou asked. She didn't dare stare at Harmony, who was pacing again behind her sister, but she knew if she had any chance of getting out of this, it was going to be with the younger Lofall sister's assistance.

"Why not kill him?" Mariah snorted. "He was a pain in everyone's side. And he was going to cost everyone more money while pocketing a boatload of his own if I didn't take him out."

"But he's been a thorn in your side for years. Why now? Was it really because of the BBS?"

"Sure," Mariah said. "I could just see it now. If he could get away with turning this place into cutesy sewing central, it wouldn't end there. It would be something else the next year, and I didn't want to leave my sister with that kind of financial burden when we're already on thin ice." She sniffed in the direction of Godfrey's home. "Not all of us who are retired are still owners of companies. We're on fixed incomes and can't add frivolities to the mix."

"But it was your handkerchief," Lou said. "Didn't you worry that it would lead back to you?"

Mariah scoffed, "No one knows anything about me. No one asks. Heck, the only person I talk to outside of my sister is my neighbors, and that's just when I see them at the mailboxes."

Neighbors. Diana Crane. Lou remembered how Easton said only a few close friends knew about her plans to meet with the corporate representative.

"You knew Diana was flying home early."

Squinting, Mariah said, "She might've let that slip during one of our conversations. We have coffee together at least once a week."

Mariah must've been the neighbor Diana had been

meeting with the day Peanut Butter barked at her in the coffee shop. He must've smelled Mariah on Diana and connected it with the handkerchief.

As Lou put that together, Mariah winced as if she realized how bad the situation had gotten. Or was it something more?

Lou hadn't spent years as an editor, dissecting sentences written by talented authors, to let something so blatant slide by. *I didn't want to leave my sister with that kind of financial burden.* Lou studied the sisters. They were probably in their seventies, like Silas, but that was far from dead, especially if they were in good health. But as Lou's detail-oriented brain looked closer at Mariah, she noticed that the two sisters, so alike in so many ways, were not alike in appearance.

Whereas Harmony's cheeks were rosy and plump, Mariah's seemed drawn and sunken. She'd tried to make up the difference with blush, but it only stood out against the natural color in her sister's similar countenance.

Mariah wasn't well.

"How long have you been sick?" Lou asked quietly.

Harmony froze in her tracks, her attention cutting from Lou to her sister. "What?"

Mariah set her jaw, anger deepening in her blue eyes.

"You're worried about your sister's financial state once you're gone, and you took care of the one thing standing in her way of being comfortable, didn't you?" Lou watched Mariah.

The older sister only simmered in complete and utter hatred.

Harmony ran around the couch to sit next to her sister, Hermeowone still resting happily in her arms. "Mariah, what's she talking about? You're fine. Right?"

Mariah peeled her hateful gaze from Lou, softening as she looked at her sister. "I have cancer, Harmony."

"But you can go through treatment and—"

Mariah held up a hand to stop her sister's protestations. "It's stage four. Inoperable. That's all you need to know. I wasn't about to stick you with a bunch of medical bills you'd be paying off long after I was gone."

Tears slipped down Harmony's cheeks, and she shook her head, sinking her fingers into the cat's fur.

"There was a part of you that wanted to get caught, wasn't there?" Lou asked, unsure where she was going with that, but knowing she needed to get Harmony on her side.

"Sure," Mariah admitted. "My sister not having to watch me wither away would've been preferable, so even if I got caught..." She opened her hands.

"No." Harmony sobbed. "You can apologize. Say it was an accident."

"Harm, it wasn't an accident. I knew Diana was flying home early, but not telling Godfrey. I knew he was fighting with Brock. I knew there would be a dozen people before me who would be suspects if he turned up dead." Mariah exhaled with fatigue. "I planned it all out so he couldn't bother you anymore, especially not once I'm gone."

Hermeowone turned toward the other sister, as if judging her for what she'd just divulged.

"And as much as I love the idea of you having a

companion once I'm gone," Mariah said as she gestured to the cat, "you cannot keep that one."

"Why?" Harmony gulped in air as she clutched the animal closer.

"Everyone knows it belonged to Lou. I can't have anything pointing to her coming here today. Not if I'm going to get rid of her." Mariah's tone was calm as she laid out her plan.

Harmony, who'd been concerned about her sister until that moment, snapped her gaze to Lou. "Get rid of her?" she asked, her tone turning cold. "No. You can't."

But she could, Lou realized. No one knew where Lou was at the moment. She'd forgotten about bringing Herme-owone to the Lofalls' today, and so she hadn't told anyone else where she was going.

Mariah turned to her sister with the most compassion Lou had seen in the killer. "Oh, Harmony. Please don't be so naïve. What else did you think was going to happen when I hit her over the head and tied her up?" Mariah snorted.

It wasn't as if Lou was naïve. She'd known it wasn't looking good for her the moment she'd woken up, bound to the chair. But Mariah talking about it so openly lit a fire in Lou, kick-starting the part of her brain that she would need to plan a way out of this. Harmony might be upset with her sister, but she also seemed incapable of going against her, which meant Lou couldn't count on her to help.

Moving her wrists, she noticed they weren't tied all that tightly. The sisters must not have had any rope in the house, and it felt like Mariah had used an electrical cord to tie her hands together. Which meant she had some wiggle room.

She started moving her wrists from side to side, stretching the cord. But Lou would need to buy herself some time if she was going to free herself completely. Scanning the room for anything she could comment on, Lou noticed that Mariah's hands shook where she sat. She was weak. Hitting Lou over the head with whatever she'd used and tying her up must've taken all her strength.

"How'd you wrestle Godfrey's gun from him?" Lou asked, pausing her wrist movement as the killer's eyes swung to her.

Mariah snorted. "I didn't need to. I watched through my bedroom window as he threatened Sasha with it when she came around to his back porch, and then he left it on the railing once she left." Mariah's gaze wandered over to her sister as she told the story.

Lou took that opportunity to work the ties from her hands, even moving her feet back and forth to work on those bonds as well.

"Stupid man," Mariah continued. "All I had to do was creep over, wait until the construction crew was at its loudest, and call him outside. Once he was dead, I wiped off my fingerprints and placed the gun back in his hands."

She turned back toward Lou, who froze. She needed more time, but Mariah was already standing. She held her arms out toward her sister.

"Now, come on," Mariah crooned. "Give me that cat, and we can get this place cleaned up."

Harmony spun her body away, protecting the cat. "You

can't take her. She trusts me. She doesn't trust anyone. And what are you going to do to Lou?"

"I figured we have enough sleeping pills in this place. I'll need your help to get her back to that bookshop of hers." Mariah tapped her fingers on her lip.

With the sisters focused on one another, Lou moved her feet and hands with more vigor, still staying as quiet as she could. But when Mariah reached for Hermeowone, and the cat hissed and swatted at her, Lou took that as her chance. She thrashed, pushing with all her might until her wrists slipped free.

"Ouch!" Mariah screamed, clutching her hand.

She lunged for the cat again, but this time, Hermeowone wriggled from Harmony's arms and launched herself toward the floor. The moment she hit the ground, she darted into the next room.

Lou brought her arms around to the front, grasping at the bonds on her ankles. Glancing up, Lou locked eyes with Harmony, whose gaze narrowed. Lou couldn't tell if that was anger or determination. She ripped at the cord, feeling it loosen the moment Mariah noticed what her sister was looking at and turned toward her.

She wouldn't have time. Mariah took a step forward. She was only a yard away.

But before Mariah could reach her, Harmony surged forward, wrapping her arms around her sister. Mariah screamed and struggled to loosen her sister's grip, but she was weakened from her disease and couldn't break free.

With the extra seconds, Lou slid her feet free of the bonds and stood.

"Go get help, Lou," Harmony yelled, breathing hard as she fought to contain her sister's twisting body.

Lou felt her pockets, but her phone was missing. Unsure where Mariah had put it, Lou wasn't about to leave Harmony alone. She couldn't be sure if Mariah would hurt her sister or not. But she'd seen a landline in the other room. It was a cordless model, sitting in a charging dock on the kitchen counter. Racing for that, Lou grabbed it and ran back into the front room as she dialed 9-1-1. She wanted to cry out in relief as the sound of the dial tone met her ears.

The moment the dispatcher picked up, Lou blurted out, "We need police in Button, in the Forrest Pond neighborhood, at house number—" She looked at Harmony.

"Three twenty-three," Harmony supplied.

Lou repeated it. "We have a murderer in custody." She moved to help Harmony, but noticed that all the fight had left Mariah.

The killer slumped against her sister, sobbing in the release that came with knowing she'd been caught.

Harmony rubbed her sister's back, and as Lou waited for the police to show, Mariah's cries filled the room, along with the repeated phrase, "I just wanted you to be okay once I was gone."

CHAPTER 24

Cars screeched to a halt in front of the Lofall house. Easton raced inside, a stream of officers following closely behind. They swarmed the Lofall sisters while Easton stayed with Lou, noticing how she cradled her head.

"Are you hurt?" His eyes scanned over her.

She blinked. "Mariah hit me over the head, but I wasn't out for long. I think I'm okay. Just a little dizzy."

Looking over his shoulder, Easton called to one of the paramedics. "Doug, can you check Lou for a head injury?"

The paramedic came over as Easton moved over to where Harmony was telling the story of everything that had happened. Lou was proud of the determination behind her steady voice and set shoulders, but she could only imagine how difficult it was to tell them the truth behind what her sister had done.

"Let's get her out of here." Easton snapped his fingers to

the officers who'd handcuffed Mariah. "Put her in the holding cell while I get Harmony's and Lou's statements."

EASTON TALKED to Harmony while Lou went through the health check with the paramedics. When she got the all clear, and was told more times than she could count how lucky she was that she didn't have a concussion, Easton was waiting for her.

She went through everything, trying not to leave out a single detail.

"Thanks, Lou. I'm so sorry we didn't catch her before she got to you." Easton exhaled. "To be honest, we weren't even close."

Lou shook her head. "Neither was I until I came here."

Sensing they were done, Harmony walked into the room. Hermeowone was in her arms, purring and rubbing her head against Harmony's chin. She crept forward.

"I would understand if you don't think this is a suitable place for her to live. I didn't even realize what my sister had done." Shame flattened Harmony's normally light tone.

Lou studied the cat, so happy even after Mariah had come after her and the house had been full of emergency personnel.

"I think this would be a great home for her, Harmony." Lou grinned. "She really seems to love you, and I know you'll take care of her."

Harmony's face lit up, and she held the cat even tighter. "Oh, thank you! I will. I'll take such good care of her."

"I can have Noah come by tomorrow with the adoption paperwork, but after everything you went through today, I think you should keep her here with you in the meantime."

Harmony proceeded to show Lou all the new stuff she'd bought to prepare for the cat.

So, by the time Lou walked out the front door an hour later, she was more than ready to go home. The crisp November air was more than welcome. And all she wanted was to find Noah and sink into his arms.

Checking her watch, she realized it was just about time for their dinner together. Shooting off a quick text to George and Willow, Lou explained her afternoon, and that she would give them more details soon, but that she had somewhere to be.

Willow responded first.

> I'll get all the details from Easton, so go. Good luck with Marigold. Stop by after if you have a moment so I can hug you.

Lou wondered how George would react, knowing the secret between them had been forgiven, but wondering if there would still be any strain on their relationship.

But then she responded, making Lou smile.

> Lou's not going to be able to be hugged after Marigold crushes all the bones in her body with her excitement. Glad you're okay, though, Lou.

That taken care of, Lou drove to Noah's house. She knocked, but there wasn't an answer. Heading inside, she found the living room empty. The place was spotless, smelled like garlic and peppers and fall spices, and Marigold's favorite album was playing through the speakers, filling the house.

Voices spilled out from the kitchen, Noah and Marigold chattering away, laughing, and talking through the steps of plating the meal they'd obviously prepared together.

Lou stopped in the doorway to the kitchen, unable to keep the grin from her face as she took them in. They were both wearing pink aprons that held the Material Girls logo from Noah's family's quilt shop, just like he'd been wearing the very first time Lou had seen Noah. Green sauce was splattered over Noah's apron, but Marigold was spotless.

At that moment, Noah glanced up, noticing she was there. His brown eyes locked on to hers, crinkling in the corners as they lit up at the sight of her. The dimples in his cheeks deepened, and he placed a hand on Marigold's shoulder.

"Our guest of honor is here," he announced.

Marigold whirled around, grinning as big as Lou had ever seen. She raced over to her, wrapping her arms around Lou in such a tight hug, Lou was sure George hadn't been exaggerating.

"We made pozole! It's soup, and it's my favorite." Marigold tugged Lou's hand as she led her into the kitchen.

"Abuela's recipe," Noah added as he dipped his head in confirmation. But as Lou came closer to him, pulled forward by his daughter, Noah seemed to recognize the fatigue on her features. "Everything okay?" He wiped his hands, stepping toward her.

Lou blinked, not sure what to say. "Everything's good now, but I had a long day." She didn't want to go into all the details in front of Marigold, knowing she would worry about Lou if she heard how close she'd gotten to a killer, yet again. "Let's just say Godfrey's case is closed."

Noah held her gaze but left it for now, knowing she would fill him in later. "Well, have a seat. We're just about ready here."

"Yes, Lou, I made you a special seat." Marigold's small hand tugged at hers again as she moved her through the kitchen and into the attached dining room.

Lou found a place setting, complete with construction paper flowers and a drawing Marigold had made for her. It was all so sweet, and if Lou didn't already know that this was just how lovely the girl was all the time, she would've guessed that Noah already told her what they were supposed to discuss that evening.

Noah followed behind with two steaming bowls of soup. Marigold bustled off to grab the last one. There were a few more trips into the kitchen to grab the toppings and a pitcher of water for the table.

After such a long day, Lou sank back into the chair, reveling in the warmth of the home she was in, as well as her company. The two Rameros sitting across from her were some of her very favorite people in the whole world. It was wild to her to think that two years ago, she hadn't even known them. But wasn't that how life worked?

She thought about Ben, and she wasn't sure if he was watching over her in that moment or if she just knew he would want her to be happy, but she felt his support as she moved on to yet another great love in her life. Lou's eyes settled on Marigold. Make that loves. Because she knew, as fast as she was falling for Noah, that little girl had her heart since the moment she'd met her.

They dug into their food, eating as they questioned Marigold about the science fair.

"Oh, I'm not sure if you've talked to Ruby, but Cass told me the good news." Noah's dark eyes danced with excitement.

Lou shook her head, urging him to go on.

"Diana is having Cass put her house on the market, and she finally agreed to let Ruby buy the Bean and Button." Noah set down his spoon.

A lightness filled Lou's heart. "I'm so happy. Ruby deserves it."

It was nice to know that things had turned out okay in the end, even if it had been a rocky road to arrive there.

They moved on to other topics as they ate: the progress on George's floors, how Noah had talked to a company about replacing Lou's window, and how happy Sebastian was to finally have his editor-in-chief hired. Once their bowls were empty and their bellies full, Noah glanced over at Lou. A slight raise of his eyebrows was the only question Lou needed. She gave a nod of agreement.

"Goldie, we've got something to talk to you about." Noah folded his napkin and set it on the table.

Marigold was a blur as she jumped out of her chair, wrapping her arms around Noah first. "Omigosh, it *is* true," she squealed out the words as she let go of Noah and raced around to squeeze Lou.

Noah swallowed, frowning at his daughter. "What's true?" he asked cautiously.

Marigold snorted. "That you and Lou are finally *a thing*," she said, as if it was as clear as the window next to them.

Lou and Noah blinked at one another.

Marigold put a hand on her hip. "Dad, I've known Lou was the one for you since she moved here, but I thought you were too silly to see it."

Noah's mouth moved from gaping to a curling a smile.

"And then, lately, you've started saying her name differently. I don't know what it is about it, but I knew you'd changed your mind." She turned to Lou and grinned. "And it's true!"

Lou let out a whoosh of air as Marigold hugged her even tighter than before. But all Lou could do was laugh, wrap her arms around the girl, and hug back. "She's got you there, Noah. We could've saved this whole thing if you'd told me you'd been saying my name differently for months."

Noah chuckled, running a hand over his face. "I guess so." His eyes sparkled with happiness. "Goldie, I want you to know that we've already told your mom, but we wanted to wait and tell you before we became official with the town."

"And Mom was okay?" Marigold's gaze flicked to Lou. "I mean, I know she loves Lou, and I know she wants what's best for you, Dad..."

Noah beamed. "She was happy. Not as ecstatic as you, but happy."

Marigold's shoulders slumped forward in relief. "I can't believe I have the best dad and two of the best moms." She wandered back to her chair in a happy daze.

The declaration jolted through Noah, and he glanced at Lou, as if he was worried that his daughter's wording would scare her off.

But Lou wasn't fazed. It was why they'd waited after all. They knew Marigold loved with every part of herself, and when she found out, there was no going back. Lou might not have a ring on her finger, but she was a part of this family now.

The certainty in her expression must've shown Noah exactly what she was feeling, because he smiled.

"You really are the luckiest," he said. "We all are that Lou decided to move here."

"Can we watch a movie?" Marigold asked, clapping her hands as if she already knew they were going to say yes.

The adults agreed, and they moved into the living room once dinner was cleared.

There, tucked onto the couch in between Noah and Marigold, Lou's heart felt the fullest it had since she'd lost Ben. And she knew not everyone got a second chance at happiness, but she was so grateful that she had, and that hers was in Button.

WHISKERS AND WORDS WILL RETURN ...

Book 9 - A Bad Feline
Things just got *purrsonal*.

February unleashes a whirlwind of surprises in the charming town of Button, Washington. While Lou preps the bookshop for another Valentine's Day, Willow has her hands full with the needy new renters next door who seem to be experts in conjuring up problems from thin air. Just when Willow's convinced they're master manipulators, a chilling phone call shatters her skepticism – a lifeless body has been discovered in their very own backyard.

The dilemma deepens as the current tenants, already teetering on the brink of moving out, demand immediate attention. The twist? The deceased was none other than a prospective tenant Willow and Easton had recently turned away, their instincts screaming that he was the wrong kind of neighbor. But it turns out that the bad feeling they got about the man might've been more of an omen of what was to come. As connections between Easton, Willow, and the deceased continue to add up, Lou and Noah jump in to help their friends. What should have been a season dedicated to love becomes veiled in an intricate tapestry of mystery and deception, with each step leading them further into danger.

Get your copy!

Join Eryn Scott's mailing list to learn about new releases and sales!

ALSO BY ERYN SCOTT

STONEYBROOK MYSTERIES

Ongoing series * Farmers market * Recipes * Crime solving twins * Cats!

A MURDER AT THE MORRISEY MYSTERY SERIES

Ongoing series * Friendly ghosts * Quirky downtown Seattle building

Pebble Cove Teahouse Mysteries

Completed series * Friendly ghosts * Oregon Coast * Cat mayors

Whiskers and Words Mysteries

Ongoing series * Best friends *
Bookshop full of cats

PEPPER BROOKS
COZY MYSTERY SERIES

Completed series * Literary mysteries * Sweet romance * Cute dog

About the Author

Eryn Scott lives in the Pacific Northwest with her husband and their quirky animals. She loves classic literature, musicals, knitting, and hiking. She writes cozy mysteries and women's fiction.

Join her mailing list to learn about new releases and sales!

www.erynscott.com